D1741528

SCORCH--A SCI-FI ALIEN WARRIOR ROMANCE

INFERNO FORCE OF THE DREXIAN WARRIORS #2

TANA STONE

BROADMOOR BOOKS

For my all the fabulous readers in Tana Stone's Tributes. You make every day a party!

xoxo

Tana

CHAPTER
ONE

Samaira

The hard jolt of the spaceship touching down in the hangar bay woke me, and I snapped my head up, glancing around to see if anyone had noticed that I'd nodded off. Luckily, the Drexian warriors piloting the shuttle were focused on landing, and not on the passenger strapped into one of the bench seats behind them.

I ran a hand through my bushy bob, glad for once that my dark hair was thick and needed little primping. Not that I would have bothered, anyway. I might be working with the Drexians, but that did not mean I had any desire to become one of their tribute brides. Even if I had just landed on the newest space station devoted to human brides and their alien mates.

"We've arrived at the Island," one of the pilots said, as

the engines powered down and the back hatch lowered behind me.

I stifled the urge to snort out a laugh at the name of the station. I'd thought it was strange enough that the Drexians had called their original space station the Boat after the old TV show *The Love Boat,* but I'd chalked it up to the fact that they'd built the thing over thirty years earlier. But now they'd gone and named the new one the Island after the equally dated and arguably cheesier TV show, *Fantasy Island.* To be honest, I hadn't watched either show. They were considered old well before I was born, and since I'd grown up in East London, vintage American TV hadn't been my thing.

I peered out the back hatch as I unfastened my safety straps, my eyes adjusting from the sleek ebony interior of the transport ship to the bright openness of the hangar bay. "Someone must have a real hard-on for 70s and 80s shows."

"What was that?" The other Drexian swiveled his head to face me.

"Nothing." I stood and retrieved my pack from an inset storage cabinet, pressing the shiny, black wall to pop it open. "I guess I didn't expect the Island to look like a regular vessel."

The Drexians exchanged a quick glance. "This is only the hangar bay, and it's one of the few parts of the station that isn't augmented with holographic technology."

Since the Drexians had revealed themselves to humanity in what was commonly called The Big Reveal, I'd seen interviews with some of the tribute brides who'd been living on the alien space station for years. They'd described holographic environments that were beyond anything we'd been able to create on Earth, but so far, I hadn't witnessed the technology for myself.

"Is that your way of saying 'you haven't seen anything yet, love?'" I quipped, before striding down the ramp and off the transport ship.

Pausing at the bottom, I inhaled the pungent scent of engine fuel. I tipped my head back to peer at the exposed beams high in the soaring ceiling as huge Drexians in dark uniforms with medal-laden sashes crossing their chests or equally impressive flight suits hurried past. Another glossy, black ship—this one with a long nose and a single cockpit on top—blasted through the opening at the far end of the hangar bay, the energy forcefield rippling as the ship touched down and skidded to a stop.

Even without holographic technology, the alien space station and all the ships were impressive. I'd gotten used to flying on the sleek Drexian vessels, and I'd even adjusted to the strange sensation of jumping through space to cross vast distances in an instant, but for a girl who'd grown up in a shabby council house, the gleaming metal and advanced alien technology was a big change.

"Are you the only one?"

The clipped voice startled me and forced me to bring my gaze down—then down even farther still, when I realized the individual speaking was only half my height. His stature wasn't even close to his most notable feature, though. The little alien had spiky, purple hair along with big, round eyes, and wore a lime-green suit, with velvet lapels and flared pants.

He tapped one white, platformed toe when I didn't answer, cutting his gaze to the creature who'd bustled up next to him, a willowy female with pale-gray skin and a swath of blue hair that extended straight up in a gravity-defying swirl and must have made her easily twice the tiny alien's height.

"I told you they shouldn't stop transporting them in stasis, Reina." He waved his stubby fingers at me. "This one looks like she's got space daze."

"She looks fine to me." The tall alien's voice was high and breathy as she gave me a wide smile. "Don't mind Serge. He's in a state."

Serge huffed out an impatient breath. "Of course, I'm in a state. We're supposed to be getting tribute brides, but the station is in an uproar because of that missing pilot."

The alien he'd called Reina frowned. "Poor Jax. You can't blame the captain for insisting on devoting all the station resources to finding him and getting him back."

Serge's tapping ceased. "Not at all. I'm as fond of Jax as anyone. I had my eye on him as one of my future grooms." He sighed. "But that's neither here nor there. Let's focus on the matter at hand."

"Who are you two?" I managed to say, as Serge began to circle me, drumming his fingers on his chin.

"I'm Reina." She extended one bony hand to me. "And this is Serge. We're here to help make your transition onto the station as easy as possible."

Despite the quirky name for the station, I'd expected my alien intelligence liaisons to be a bit less flamboyant. I was here for a military mission after all.

"Tall and athletic," Serge mused, as he finished circling me and crossed his arms. "That's an easy sell. Gorgeous skin

—and are those eyelashes real?" He leaned closer. "Of course, they are. And what species are you, sweetie?"

"Species?"

"Ethnicity," Reina said with a giggle. "He always mixes that up."

I folded my arms across my chest to match the little alien's stance. "Not that it matters, but I'm British. Pakistani, if you're going to get specific about it."

"Pakistani," Serge said, almost reverently. "How wonderful. I've never worked with a Pakistani tribute before."

I stared at him for a beat as the word sunk in. "Tribute? As in tribute bride?"

Serge went back to rapping his toe on the hard floor. "Please tell me we aren't back to this again." He gave Reina a tortured look. "I thought all the new brides were volunteers. How did one slip through who doesn't know what she signed up for?"

I held up both palms and shook my head. "I promise you, I'm not a tribute bride. I know all about the program, and it's the last thing for which I would ever volunteer."

One of the Drexian pilots I'd traveled with thundered down the metal ramp of the ship behind me. "She's telling the truth. She's not here to be matched."

Serge threw his hands in the air. "Then why is a beautiful Earth woman being transported onto the Island?"

"She didn't have much of a choice."

We all turned as another Drexian, this one with long, dark hair and a Drexian uniform emblazoned with a flame insignia on the chest, approached.

"Captain Kalex," Reina said, patches of pink appearing on her gray cheeks.

"What do you mean she didn't have much of a choice?" Serge asked, narrowing his gaze at the captain and clearly not as flustered by the brawny Drexian as Reina. "What's going on here?"

I braced myself for the captain to reveal the truth of my past and how I'd ended up on the alien space station, but instead he nodded his head at me.

"Welcome aboard, officer."

I recalled that Drexians saluted by thumping one fist across their chests, so I gave him my best salute. "Thank you, Captain. It's good to be here."

He returned my salute, then pivoted to the two aliens gaping at me. "Samaira has been sent by Earth to join the mission to rescue Jax."

"Actually, I go by Sam," I said, not adding that the only person who still called me Samaira was my father, whom I hadn't laid eyes on in years.

Serge wrinkled his nose and muttered something about peculiar human names for females.

Reina's eyes widened. "Are you in the military, hon, I mean, Sam?"

Even though she was an alien, and I was standing on a space station light years away from Earth, I hesitated at revealing that I'd been recruited by MI-6 to join the elite human-Drexian intelligence team. And if I wasn't going to tell her that, I certainly wasn't going to reveal that I'd been offered the choice of joining the team or going to prison for a long time. That wasn't exactly the kind of thing you casually dropped into a conversation.

"Earth agreed to send her to us because she has specialized skills," the captain said, before I could sidestep the question. "Skills we're going to need if we're going to get Jax away from the Kronock."

"How exciting," Reina said, giving me a pat on the arm. "Even though you aren't going to be one of our brides, if you need anything while you're on the station, feel free to ask, hon."

Serge groaned. "I'm not going to say I'm not crushed." Then he also patted my arm, although more brusquely. "I still maintain that you'd make a spectacular bride, sweetie. You change your mind, you come talk to me. I could have the Drexian warriors lining up faster than a hot knife through butter."

When I stared at Serge, Reina giggled. "He loves his Earth sayings."

"I'm not sure what part of Earth that's from," I said under my breath," but it's not London." Then I gave them both as genuine a smile as I could muster. "Thanks."

I will never change my mind, I thought to myself.

"Let's go." Kalex motioned with his head for me to follow him. "I need to brief you on the mission."

I wasn't short, but I had to walk fast to keep up with the captain's long strides as we left the hangar bay and entered the attached corridor. Instantly, the exposed beams and scent of burning fuel was replaced by curved white walls and a lower ceiling. At the end of the corridor, we stepped into what appeared to be an elevator compartment, the doors gliding closed behind us. Pink light pulsed and Muzak played in the background as we rose, and then the compartment swiveled and began traveling sideways.

Captain Kalex spun to face me, his expression severe. "I know about you."

I met his gaze, my heart racing and my mouth going dry. Shit. So much for being able to outrun my problems. Even thousands of kilometers away from Earth, my past was chasing after me. Not that I should have expected a clean slate. That hadn't been part of the deal. "I assumed you would have read my file."

"Deception is not tolerated within the Drexian code of honor."

I knew enough about the alien race to know that they prided themselves on honor and duty, especially the ones who joined Inferno Force. I flicked my gaze to the flame insignia on his uniform. "It's not tolerated on Earth, either. That's why I was headed to prison."

He grunted. "But now you're here. Why?"

I crossed my arms and cocked my head at him. "If you read my file, you wouldn't be asking me that." I didn't mean to be snarky, but it was my first reaction when cornered.

"You're a criminal."

I bristled at that coarse description. I was so much more than a thief. "Like I said, if you read my entire file you would know I'm one of the best thieves on the planet. I can break into anywhere and lift the most well-guarded treasures without a trace."

A muscle ticked in his jaw as he studied me. "I won't tolerate criminal behavior on my station."

I laughed, the sound echoing in the small compartment. "There's nothing on this station I'd want to steal." I pivoted to face the doors. "Besides, I only steal from those who steal from others."

"What does that mean?"

Heat suffused my cheeks as I thought about the wealthy

I'd stolen from on Earth. "I only rob bad people who deserve a little punishment the world will never otherwise give them. Which means I won't be stealing from the Drexians." I swiveled my head back to him. "You're the good guys, right?"

He slatted his eyes as he appraised me. It was clear he wasn't used to officers like me. "Right."

"Then I'm only going to steal from the aliens who took something that doesn't belong to them."

"The Kronock," Captain Kalex said, his voice raspy and rough.

I nodded, a thrill going through me at the thought of stealing the missing Drexian warrior back from the aliens who'd tried to invade Earth. Like with all my jobs, I would be exacting my own form of revenge. "The Kronock."

CHAPTER
TWO

Jaxon

The light shone bright in my eyes, but I didn't open them. There was no point.

The only time the crushing darkness of my cell was replaced with light was when the Kronock guards came to drag me to the interrogation chamber, and I'd already memorized every dread-filled step down the dank hall.

"Get up!"

The guttural sound of the Kronock voice didn't even startle me anymore, although I wished that my universal translator implant didn't work so well. I hated understanding every vile word the creatures spoke and every vicious threat they made.

Despite the harsh command coming from the doorway of my cell, I ignored it. It hadn't taken me long to learn that my abuse wasn't linked to how well I obeyed commands. The beasts would torture me regardless of how quickly I moved, so I allowed myself to linger a few more moments on the iron bench that served as my bed.

If I squeezed my eyes tightly enough, I could almost imagine that I was back on the space station or, even better, at the Drexian military academy. Instead of the raspy breaths of the scaled creature hulking toward me, I recalled the sounds of cheers as I sparred with my fellow cadets in the battle ring, slashing with the traditional Drexian blades that were as curved and sharp as the ridge on a Gantherian water dragon.

Then my muddled mind drifted to the time I'd fought a Gantherian water dragon on an Inferno Force mission, the violent sea monster almost dragging half of my unit down to the depths of an icy sea before we'd slayed him. I could almost feel the frigid water sluicing off my skin as I'd hoisted myself onto the frozen surface, prickles erupting across my flesh from the wind.

"I said, get up, Drexian scum!"

The sound jerked me from my memories and back to reality, where the prickles on my skin were real and from the chill that had seeped into it. I opened my eyes, flinching and lifting an arm to cover them. Then I flinched again, the movement of my arm sending a sharp pain ricocheting through my body.

My medical training was rudimentary and had been a long time ago, but I suspected I had at least two bruised ribs—if they weren't broken entirely. Breathing anything but small, shallow breaths was painful. Not that my injuries would prevent the Kronock from torturing me further.

"I'm coming, handsome," I drawled, enjoying the growl my response elicited.

If there was one thing I'd confirmed during my time as a captive of my enemy, it was that the Kronock had no limit to their cruelty—and no sense of humor. That didn't stop me from mocking them. It was one of the ways I could remind myself that they hadn't broken me.

Pushing myself up to a sitting position, I gritted my teeth before I stood. As an Inferno Force warrior, I'd learned to endure extreme battle conditions and even deprivation of food and water. But I'd never been subjected to day after day of Kronock torture before.

I didn't even know how many days had passed since I'd been taken captive. Not only was my ship's capture a blur, but my mind remained muddled from the lack of sleep. As soon as I'd stop shivering long enough to drift off, the lights would come on, and I'd be dragged down for more inter-rogation.

The enormous Kronock guard stomped over, his thick tail dragging across the floor, and took me by the arm, jerking me toward him. "You have a date with the bone worker, *handsome.*"

A chill went through me, but I forced myself to laugh. "He must have a real name. After all our time together, I feel like I should call him something less formal."

The Kronock grunted, clearly not pleased by my banter as he half walked/half dragged me from the cell and down the corridor. Making light of the situation was the only way I could keep myself sane. That and the unmistakable knowl-edge that my Drexian brothers would come for me.

I thought of Kalex, who had served with me on Captain

Brok's Inferno Force battleship. He'd been with me when I'd been taken. Both of our ships had been racing toward the rift in space that would take us back to Drexian space. I'd watched his ship fly through and had been right behind him when my ship had been blasted and the rift had vanished. After that, everything had gone black. I'd woken up in a Kronock cell with no concept of whether I was on a battleship or one of their planets.

"It doesn't matter," I muttered to myself, the scraping of my feet on the dirty iron floors masking my words. My Drexian brothers would find me. I just had to stay alive long enough.

I glanced up as the Kronock slowed, and I recognized the arched doorway ahead. My blood ran cold at the thought of what was beyond it, and I instinctively braced my feet to slow our movement.

"I thought you liked Zakrov," the Kronock said, letting out his version of a laugh, which sounded like a raspier belch.

A glimmer of satisfaction flared within me. *Zakrov.* The alien torturer was called Zakrov. I repeated the name over and over in my head, as we lurched toward the bone worker's lair. The more information I could take back to my people, the easier it would be to destroy the Kronock.

We'd already crippled their operations by destroying their labs and confiscating data. Even their military power had been considerably weakened during their failed attack on Earth. I suspected the creatures were desperately trying to cobble together what ships and soldiers remained. Either they were planning more attacks on my people, or they were going to retreat until they'd amassed enough of a force to come for us again. One thing I knew for certain—they would never give up their attempts to control the galaxy and destroy the Drexians.

"You're right," I said as the guard pushed me through the doorway. "We're old friends."

Zakrov the bone worker stood on the other side of a metal reclining chair, the straps that would soon bind my arms and legs hanging limply from the sides. He shared the same gray scales as all Kronock, as well as the clawed hands and feet, but he was not as massive as the warriors I'd battled in the past.

Since the Kronock had emerged from their dormancy not long ago, we'd learned that they'd been engaged in genetic modifications in the decades they'd been quiet, creating versions of their species for fighting and others for commanding. This smaller version, with a bulbous forehead over his elongated jaw, appeared to be the most intelligent of the species—a scientist of sorts, although his specialty seemed to be torture. His bionic implant covered half of his head, the red eye blinking rapidly, as he eyed me like a starving predator.

"Are we friends?" The torturer rasped, his one beady eye darting from me to the guard braced in front of the door.

I didn't respond, my skin icing at the sight of a tray of electrodes next to Zakrov. I could feel the scorch marks on my skin without even touching them, the skin still raw from my last session.

"If we were friends, you'd tell me about your new station and your arrangement with those puny aliens," Zakrov spat.

"I'd hate to spoil our relationship by moving too quickly," I said, forcing myself give him my most charming smile.

He curled one of his clawed hands into a gnarled fist. "Maybe you'll change your mind after I attach these electrodes to those intriguing bumps on your back."

I willed myself not to react, although I knew how painful it would be to have my nodes seared with electricity. They were one of the most sensitive parts of a Drexian's body— usually used for arousal. But it didn't matter. I'd never give up information about my people.

As the guard jabbed me hard from behind, forcing me to stumble closer to Zakrov, I steeled myself to the impending pain and thought about Kalex and Vekron. If anyone could get me out, it was them.

If only they made it in time.

CHAPTER
THREE

Samaira

I swiped my fingers across the tablet, as I absently picked at my food. Aliens bustled around me, although I'd selected a table wedged in the corner of the space station's staff canteen solely so I wouldn't be disturbed. The din of conversation didn't bother me, nor did the cacophony of pungent smells from the alien food—and the various aliens themselves. I'd always been able to tune out distractions, which was one of the reasons I was so good at what I did.

I'd have to be brilliant to pull off this job, I thought with a heavy sigh as I peered at the screen.

I'd only been on the Drexian space station for a few hours, but I'd already learned that the captain didn't trust me, and the aliens with nubby horns and long tails were like horny teenagers. Luckily, the Neebix had stopped making eyes at me when I'd flashed them the middle finger and a few cold stares.

I suspected my gesture wouldn't have been considered proper alien-human interaction since the Drexians—and their allies—were supposed to be our allies, but I wasn't there to make friends. I was on a job, and I hated to be distracted when I was prepping for a job. And I especially hated to be hit on.

One more thing I'd learned since arriving on the Island? My mission was most likely a death sentence.

I suppressed the urge to throw the tablet across the room, even though it would probably be just as helpful in shards as it was to me now. Captain Kalex had given me all the information they had on the Kronock ship I'd be sneaking onto, and the schematics weren't exactly like the blueprints I usually used in researching a target. For one thing, they were incomplete, with gaps in the plans that he said was a result of the data being corrupted as it was retrieved. Okay, that I could work around.

But most worrying was that the schematics weren't current. The captain admitted that the plans he had for the Kronock battleships—the ones I'd been staring at—were over a year old, and he suspected the aliens had made modifications since the information had been obtained by the Drexians.

"Which makes this bloody useless," I mumbled to myself as I took another bite of the spicy Drexian stew that reminded me a little of *Siri paya*, although I doubted the Drexian dish contained hooves like the Pakistani version did.

"You mind if we join you?"

I glanced up, almost forgetting that I was in a busy

canteen used by all the crew. My first instinct was to tell the woman with curly, brown hair and glasses that I was busy, but the Drexian warrior standing beside her with the man bun made me reconsider. Even though he was just as big and brawny as the other Drexians I'd met, something about his searching gaze reminded me of a guy on one of my early teams, a brainy, good-looking kid who never should have been out in the field with us and never should have gotten scooped up.

I straightened and nodded to the chairs across from me then glanced back down at my tablet. "Suit yourself, but I doubt I'll be good company."

The woman slid out a chair and plopped down, resting her forearms on the table. "We know who you are. That's why we're here."

I sat back, shifting my gaze from the grinning woman in the brightly colored top to the more serious Drexian who'd now joined her at the table. The thought of total strangers knowing about me—or thinking they did—rankled me. I worked alone precisely because I didn't like people knowing about me. "What do you know?"

"I'm Nina, by the way," the woman said, holding out her hand.

I took it but didn't return her smile. I'd known plenty of people who could smile prettily while stabbing you in the back, so it was going to take more than a cute grin to win my trust. "Sam."

"Sam." The woman repeated my name, nodding. "I like it. It suits you. You're British?"

I raised an eyebrow at this.

"Your accent." Nina laughed at my obvious surprise, then added, "Which I love, by the way."

"Right, of course." I let out a breath.

Paranoid much, Sam? Anyone who'd ever heard a British accent would know where I grew up, even if they couldn't quite pinpoint what part of the U.K.

"Vekron," the Drexian said curtly. He clearly wasn't as into the small talk as the woman, which suited me just fine.

"You said you know about me?"

Nina slid her glasses up her nose. "You're the specialist who's here to join the mission to rescue Jax, aren't you?"

My shoulders relaxed a bit. So, the captain was billing me as a specialist. I guessed telling his crew that a professional thief was involved in saving their colleague might not inspire confidence. That worked for me. "That's right. I was just reviewing the schematics of the Kronock battleship."

Vekron frowned. "About that..."

"They're a bloody disaster," I finished for him, putting the tablet flat on the table.

Nina's face fell as she stared at the tablet. "What do you mean?"

"The files were corrupted," Vekron said. "Kalex showed me. I attempted to repair them but had no luck."

The woman swung her head toward him. "Why didn't you tell me? I could have tried to help."

"Big chunks of the data are missing, Nina. There's no way to salvage what isn't there."

She scowled at him, clearly disagreeing. "Still..."

I eyed the two, leaning further back in my chair. "So, are you two...?"

Nina's eyes widened behind her lenses. "Me and

Vekron?" She shook her head vehemently. "No, we're definitely not."

Vekron's brows pressed together for a beat, and it was clear he wasn't thrilled by how fervently she protested the possibility they were a couple.

"Just mates then?" I asked, amused by the dynamic and pleased it was distracting them from me.

"Definitely," Nina said. "We work together designing the holograms used on the station. Vekron does the more technical part, and I do design."

"So, you're good with computer programming?" I asked Vekron.

He twitched one shoulder. "Computers, devices, machines."

"He's kind of a tech genius," Nina said in a stage whisper. "Like, an actual genius, not one of those Apple store geniuses."

I smiled at this. The woman was growing on me. "So, he does the tech stuff after you design it?"

"Kind of, but a holographic designer has to know something about programming the system, so I'm not a total noob."

"A holographic designer," I said. "I never thought that would be an actual job."

Nina's wide grin returned. "You and me both. My cousin has been a holographic designer on the original Drexian space station for years, but, of course, no one knew about that until the Big Reveal."

Vekron cleared his throat. "About the Kronock schematics."

I straightened, focusing on the tablet again. If this

Drexian was as clever as he sounded, he might be helpful. "If you worked on the files, you know how many gaps there are. Not to mention the fact that all of this is over a year old. How am I supposed to sneak aboard an alien ship and rescue this Drexian if I can't figure out the venting systems?"

"Your mission is to sneak onto the Kronock ship?" Nina's voice was a hush.

I pressed my lips together, hoping I hadn't said too much. Regardless, I needed Vekron's help—if he could give it. "I'm not worried about getting on. From what Captain Kalex tells me, your ships have stealth shielding and your pilots are the best. I'm just used to being better prepared for what to expect once I'm on the inside."

Nina tilted her head at me, and a curl flopped over her forehead. "You aren't military, are you?"

"Not exactly."

Vekron cleared his throat, and I suspected he knew more about me than his 'definitely just a friend.' "Those schematics are the best documents we have regarding enemy battleships, but there's another way for you to figure out the insides of a Kronock ship."

"I'm all ears, mate," I told him, wondering why his captain had held out on me.

Vekron pulled out a device. "This isn't exactly protocol, but I'm Inferno Force and we've never been great at that type of thing anyway."

Now my interest was piqued. If the Drexian was suggesting something illegal or unethical, he was speaking my language. For me, operating on the outskirts of what was acceptable had always felt more comfortable.

He tapped the screen and a face appeared. It was obviously a Drexian male, but this one had short brown hair and a thin scar running along the top of his eyebrow and down one temple.

"Vox," Vekron said. "Thanks for agreeing to vid chat with us."

"Anything to help," the Drexian on the screen said. "I hear you're going after one of our warriors."

"I'm not." Vekron frowned, then pivoted the screen so that Vox could see me. "But Sam is, and she needs to know everything you do about the inside of a Kronock battleship."

I stared at the Drexian, baffled by what information he might have that would be better than schematics, even if they were damaged. "You're the one with the secret storehouse of information on Kronock battleships?" I raised an eyebrow. "You aren't secretly a Kronock, are you?"

He smiled at my weak attempt to lighten the mood. "Not anymore."

FOUR

Samaira

T leaned against the inside of the inclinator with my eyes closed. A strange, instrumental version of the *Magnum P.I.* theme song played in the background, but even that didn't distract me from running through the plan in my mind.

I'd stayed up half the night reviewing what Vox had told me about Kronock ships. After I'd gotten over my initial shock that the Drexian warrior had been held captive by the Kronock and even implanted with one of their bionic devices and their DNA, I'd realized what an invaluable resource he was. Human intelligence was always an added edge, even when it came to burglary, so knowing firsthand how the station was laid out and where the weaknesses were had made me feel more confident about the job.

"Not that it matters," I said under my breath, rubbing my

palms down my snug black pants as the inclinator slowed and the doors glided open. The mission was a go whether I was ready or not.

I opened my eyes, took a deep breath, and walked purposefully toward the hangar bay. Sure, I would have loved more time to memorize the details or even learn more about the enemy from Vox, but the captain had made it clear that every moment we wasted, was a moment of torment for the missing Drexian.

I gulped, remembering what Vox had told me about his own treatment by the Kronock and how he'd almost lost his memories and his life. If Jaxon was still alive—and I had to admit that was a big *if*—I hated thinking of him being turned into one of the monstrous Kronock. A shiver passed through me as images of the scaly beasts flashed through my head.

"Get on, get in, and get him out," I repeated to myself, although somehow I suspected it wouldn't be as easy as that.

Striding through the double doors, I paused as I entered the hangar bay. Again, it was an abrupt transition from the sleek, white corridors with arched walls to the noise and chaos of arriving and departing spaceships. I breathed in the smell of char and fuel as I spotted the captain and Vekron standing beside a shiny black ship with outstretched wings.

"Officer," Captain Kalex said when he saw me approach, frowning slightly.

Vekron showed none of the captain's wariness, giving me a grin as I joined them. "You ready?"

I smiled back. "As ready as I'll ever be."

This response didn't impress the captain and his frown deepened. "If you feel this mission is beyond your skills..."

I blew out a breath, along with the nerves that had been gathering in my chest. "Relax, mate." I slapped him on the side of one arm. "If anyone can snatch your guy out from under their noses, it's me. I've got this."

His eyebrows shot skyward, and Vekron stifled a snort of laughter behind his hand.

I held the captain's gaze for a beat. "I promise you that I'll find your guy and bring him home."

Kalex finally gave me a sharp nod, stepping aside and waving a hand at the open ramp leading onto the ship. "The pilot and your personal security guard are already onboard."

"Security guard?"

"I know you're used to," he hesitated, "working alone, but I thought you might need some firepower to get you onto the Kronock ship—or get you off."

I shrugged. "As long as I'm not expected to get the guy through the vents with me." I eyed Kalex up and down. "You blokes aren't exactly small."

"You aren't."

"Sam," Vekron said as I started up the ramp. "Once you arrive in Kronock territory, we won't have contact with you."

I'd known this, but it was still sobering to hear. "Understood. If we get in trouble, we're on our own."

"Not necessarily." Vekron held out his hand and opened it, revealing a glittering silver ring resting in his palm.

I glanced up at him. "You might just be mates, but I've got to tell you, Nina is not going to be happy about this."

The side of his mouth quirked up. "It's a homing beacon. It isn't activated because we don't want the Kronock picking up a signal unless it's an absolute necessity."

I took the ring and slipped it onto my finger. "This is a homing beacon?"

Vekron nodded. "It looks innocuous, but the signal is strong. Once you activate it, we'll be able to locate you—even in Kronock territory."

"But so will the Kronock," I said, not waiting for the answer. "So how do I activate it?"

"Three full rotations to the left while pressing on the sides. Another three back the other way to stop sending the signal."

I studied the ring, which looked like a delicate piece of jewelry and nothing more. "Pretty clever."

"I thought you'd appreciate the use of jewelry."

I looked up at him. So, he did know more about me than he'd let on, although I was confident he hadn't shared his knowledge with Nina, which I appreciated. People usually looked at me differently when they knew I was a professional thief.

"Thanks, Vekron. For everything."

He nodded and backed down the ramp.

I gave him and the captain a final glance before turning and entering the ship, the black interior instantly swallowing me.

The vessel was smaller than the one I'd arrived on, but larger than the sleek fighter jets I'd seen swooping into the hangar bay. Like all the Drexian ships I'd seen, it was entirely black inside and out, which made it even easier to be hidden when the stealth shielding was activated.

I sat down in the bucket seat behind the pilot and across from the Drexian who'd been assigned to guard me. He was broad-shouldered and clean-cut, his dark uniform making him seem even more imposing. After I strapped in, I gave him a nod, which he returned.

At least he wasn't chatty. I despised having to carry on a conversation during a job. Usually breaking into mansions required stealth and silence so it wasn't an issue, but when I'd worked jobs with teams, there always seemed to be one who liked to talk before we went quiet. I was grateful this bloke wasn't going to be one of those.

"Ready for takeoff?" the pilot asked, craning his neck back to glance at me.

"Let's crack on," I said. Then, when he gave me a blank look, I added, "Ready for takeoff."

I closed my eyes as the engine rumbled to life and the steel floor trembled beneath my feet, vibrating up my legs. I'd never minded flying, but my experience with actual space flight was still limited, and I'd never jumped through a wormhole before.

Fear wasn't something I usually experienced in my line of work. It was a liability, and it made you sloppy. Over the years, I'd trained myself to suppress the nervous flutters that I'd gotten before jobs. Breathing exercises would slow my heart rate, and eventually the calm became second nature.

Of course, nicking jewelry wasn't in the same league as creeping aboard an alien ship and attempting to rescue a valuable prisoner. Even if I'd gotten caught breaking into a rich bloke's house, the chances had been small that they would incinerate me with a laser blaster. I swallowed hard at this thought.

It didn't matter, I told myself with a shake of my head. As dangerous as this mission was, it beat spending the rest of my natural life in prison. And if I pulled it off, I'd earn my freedom or at least parole.

Get on, get in, and get him out.

I repeated the mantra in my head as the ship roared across the floor of the hangar bay and then burst out into space. Even though my eyes remained closed, I felt the slight drop as the vessel lifted off.

The comms inside the ship crackled, a voice filling the cockpit. "Energy rift detected. You're all clear."

"Entering the rift now," the pilot said.

I gripped my knees, keeping my eyes shut as we jerked forward, the ship trembling as my body was forced back into my seat. The pressure was so intense, the skin on my face felt like it was being dragged backward. Then, as soon as it had started, the force stopped and we flew forward, my safety strap keeping me from falling.

"*Grek,*" the pilot muttered.

I opened my eyes, swiveling my head toward the window that looked into space. "Bloody hell."

The massive ship in front of us was so large I couldn't see the top or bottom of it. It was just a wall of hulking, gray metal that looked like the scales of a snake—and we'd arrived almost on top of it.

"You're sure they can't see us?" I asked, my stomach doing an uncomfortable flip.

"I'm sure," the pilot said.

Then the alarms inside the ship started to scream.

CHAPTER
FIVE

Jaxon

The movement was gentle, a tickle across my chest as I lay sprawled across the floor. I usually ended up on the bed when we visited pleasure houses, but I'd been known to roll around on the floor with one or two of the delectable alien females hired to entertain and pleasure me.

The fire that had been roaring in the hearth the night before must have gone out because the chill in the room sent a shiver through me. I moaned, the ache in my side making me strain to remember what type of acrobatics had been involved.

Had I been with Felaris twins? The haze that had settled over my brain made me think I'd definitely put away a lot of Noovian whiskey. I hesitated. Or had it been Palaxian tonic? I let out another soft groan. If I'd been drinking the alien liquor that loosened inhibitions, that would explain my current brain fog—and the bruises. I'd been known to go wild on Palaxian tonic.

And if the pleasurers had also been drinking Palaxian tonic? I chuckled, wincing from the pain in my side it provoked. Then that would explain everything.

I drew in a long breath, startled at the fetid air. Pleasure houses were known for warmth and comfort and alluring aromas not the stink of sweat and feces.

I gingerly lifted a hand to my forehead to relieve the relentless pounding. This was all wrong. The darkness, the damp, the smells.

Then the movement on my chest morphed to a scurry of feet, and I jerked up, sending whatever creature flying across the room. There was a thud and a squeak and then more scuttling as it ran off.

"*Grek*!" I slapped at my chest, the feel of the tiny feet lingering on my skin.

I wasn't in a luxurious room in a pleasure house recovering from a night of Palaxian wine and raucous fucking. I was in a dank cell being held by the Kronock. I also wasn't on the floor, but I was on a bunk that was as hard as any stone.

Swinging my feet onto the floor, I braced my head in my hands. The pain I'd been experiencing hadn't been in my imagination. That was completely real, my damaged ribs making it hard to inhale without a sharp stab of pain. I touched a hand to my bare stomach, the ridges of my muscles now scored with cuts and burns.

The only positive thing I could say about Zakrov, the alien torturer they called 'bone worker,' was that he enjoyed psychological torture even more than physical torture if that could be considered a good thing. Despite his repeated threats—and even hooking electrodes to the nodes that ran down my spine—he'd yet to damage them permanently, that is, aside from some minor shocks. Instead, he seemed to enjoy torturing me with the anticipation, describing the pain in excruciating detail before he inflicted it. At this point, I almost believed I'd experienced the pain, even though he always ripped the electrodes off once my body was tensed for the shock and sweat poured off me.

"I like to save the best for last," he would say with a gurgling laugh before ordering the guard to drag me back to my cell.

I allowed my eyes to adjust to the dimness, a faraway door sending in just enough faint light so I could make out the iron bars fronting my cell and the shadows of small creatures scurrying on the floor.

"This is what you get for leaving Inferno Force," I said to myself, my deep voice echoing back to me.

I didn't care if I was talking to myself. I needed to hear something other than the furtive scampering of alien vermin. My only contact since I'd been thrown in the cell were the guards who retrieved me for my interrogation sessions, and they weren't much for small talk. Nor did they appreciate my sense of humor.

Rubbing my hands down my bare arms and wishing I still had my uniform jacket, I leaned back against the cold wall. If I hadn't left my Inferno Force posting, I would still be surrounded by my fellow Drexians and possibly recovering from a wild night in a pleasure house. I wasn't one for regrets, but I was seriously second-guessing my decision to head up the security for the new space station especially because it was the new space station meant for the tribute brides.

An involuntary growl rose from my throat. I'd sworn I'd never have anything to do with those infernal brides, and then I'd ended up in charge of security for the new station that would be devoted to housing them and their Drexian mates. That plan hadn't worked out so well.

I'd done it because my former first officer in Inferno Force had been assigned to the station as acting captain. Kalex had pulled in Vekron to serve with him, and then asked me to join them as the head of the station's security force while it was under construction. At the time, it had seemed like an honor and a chance to lead. Now, it seemed like the worst decision of my life.

I huffed out a breath. I didn't blame Kalex or Vekron. It wasn't their fault that the Drexian empire was building a massive, high-tech space station on the edges of the galaxy.

"It's those *grekking* tribute brides," I whispered darkly, the sound evaporating into the blackness around me.

If I was being honest, it wasn't their fault either. If Drexians hadn't suffered a severe shortage of females and been forced to search for genetically compatible females, we never would have located Earth and started taking women for mates. That didn't make the whole tribute bride program any easier for me to swallow, and it was hard not to think that if my fellow Drexians weren't so obsessed with the tributes and creating opulent space stations for them, the Kronock wouldn't be equally obsessed with destroying the stations. And I wouldn't have been exploring the Kronock attempts to reach the Island and ended up stuck in Kronock space and captured by the enemy.

They'd almost destroyed the Boat—the attack crippling the station and causing all its residents to abandon ship—and now they were after the Island. The human mates couldn't be worth all this, could they?

"Give me a Haralli pleasurer any day." Thinking about the pretty, winged females made my pulse quicken.

With pleasurers, you knew what you were getting. You paid for their company, and they provided an evening of carnal pleasure with no strings attached. The human females were not like that. They required seduction and romance and devotion—and even then their affection wasn't guaranteed. I'd seen my fellow Drexian warriors put themselves through hell to win the hearts of the human they loved, and for what? To stay with one female forever?

"No thanks," I grumbled. Even in my current state, I knew that was a particular torture that wasn't for me. Not anymore.

At one point, I'd been like all the others. I'd signed up for a bride and waited breathlessly to be matched with one of the small, two-breasted creatures. I'd imagined the nights we'd spend together in our fantasy suite and how I would adore her, giving up empty encounters with alien pleasurers in exchange for the devotion of my one mate.

"*Grek* that," I said darkly, memories of what had actually happened tightening my throat. The human I'd been matched with before the Big Reveal hadn't looked at being mated to an alien warrior as a good thing. According to the handlers on the Boat, she'd had one of the worst reactions they'd ever seen and had refused to entertain the possibility of a Drexian match. I never knew if she'd been shown my image, and I didn't want to know. Regardless, she hadn't stared at my image longingly like I'd stared at hers, and she hadn't poured all her hopes and dreams into a fantasy that would never exist.

I squeezed my eyes shut until they hurt. I might have let myself be wounded by a female once, but it would never happen again. I didn't care that all the new tributes were volunteers. I wanted nothing to do with human women, and the moment I was rescued I was demanding to be transferred away from the Island, so I'd never have to lay eyes on the fickle creatures again.

I opened my eyes and peered into the bleakness. Not that females should be at the forefront of my mind. I should be preparing myself for when Kalex and Vekron and the Drexian forces arrived to rescue me. *That* was something I could count on.

CHAPTER
SIX

Samaira

"What's going on?" I screamed over the wailing alarms, as the Drexian across from me unhooked himself and leapt up from his seat. "I thought you said the Kronock couldn't detect us."

"They can't," the pilot said, his fingers flying across his console. "That's the ship's way of telling me we're too close to another ship."

Within moments, the shrieking ceased.

"Blimey!" I released a breath and put a hand to my hammering heart. "The ship couldn't find a more subtle way to do that?"

The standing Drexian braced one hand on the ceiling, as the ship pivoted and hugged the hull of the enemy ship, and we slowed our speed. "We're so close I don't think they could detect us even if we didn't have stealth shielding."

He might have a point. The mammoth battleship dwarfed our smaller vessel, making me feel like we were a flea hitching a ride on a dog.

After skimming along the hull for a few minutes, the pilot let out a triumphant sound. "There's how we'll sneak in."

I followed his line of sight but didn't notice an opening in the ship. "Is it a hidden entrance?"

He shook his head. "It's a waste chute. We have so little intel about Kronock ships we had to hope we could find something like this. We knew they had to have them, but we didn't know where they'd be."

"What kind of waste?" I asked, not sure if I wanted to know the answer.

"From the size of the hatch, I'd guess solid—space trash and industrial garbage," the standing Drexian said.

At least that was better than a sewage drain. I squinted at the chute as it opened and released a metal crate that drifted, pinwheeling, out into space. "That doesn't look large enough for this ship to fit through."

"It's not." The pilot flicked a glance to me. "I'm going to attach the ship to the hull right next to the chute, and you two are going to climb inside."

I gaped at him for a moment. "I thought the Drexians had jump technology that could transport you places instantly. Unless science operates differently out here in Kronock space, we can't go outside this ship without freezing or dying from lack of oxygen."

"We do have jump technology," the pilot said, "but using it would alert the Kronock to our presence and location."

The Drexian guard pressed his hand to one of the inset cabinets in the wall, reaching inside and retrieving some folded fabric that shimmered as jet black as the interior of the vessel. "That's why we've got these."

I caught the bundle he tossed me, peering down at the shimmery fabric and rubbing my fingers across the strangely thick yet silky surface of it. "What is this?"

"An environmental suit. It will protect us from the elements and provide us with oxygen."

I glanced at him then back at the lightweight jumpsuit I'd unfurled. "This is a space suit? It looks like a superhero leotard." I held it up by the shoulders, as the fabric pooled onto the floor. "And it's way too big for me."

The Drexian security officer didn't answer, instead stepping into his own suit and clamping a cuff around one wrist. He tapped the cuff and the fabric seemed to morph to his body, whatever excess vanishing as if by magic. Almost as soon as it had shrunk to fit him, the Drexian himself appeared to vanish.

I blinked hard as only his head remained fully visible. "What in the bloody hell?"

The pilot craned his neck around, but he didn't seem fazed. "Our environmental suits have stealth shielding. I'm surprised you weren't briefed on this before we left."

"Me, too," I grumbled, stepping into my own suit. To be fair, I had cut the captain off in the middle of his long monologue about Drexian technology, thinking he was being an arrogant wanker and telling him that my job was about cunning and skill more than gadgets and tech.

Who's the wanker now? I thought with a sigh.

Once I'd fastened my suit, the security officer hooked a cuff around my wrist and tapped it so the excess fabric would shrink around my body.

When I looked down, I nearly gasped. Instead of shimmery fabric, my body seemed to have disappeared entirely. I rubbed my hands down the front of my body, my eyes needing proof that I hadn't evaporated.

Nope, I thought as my fingers skimmed the slick fabric. I was still there, but the environment suit had taken on the exact coloring of the background, so I blended completely.

The Drexian reached over and flipped a hood over my head, zipping a clear window around my face before I could protest. "The wristband controls your oxygen. Tap it twice to start the flow."

His voice was slightly muffled with the hood up, but I could still understand him, and I tapped my wristband twice. Instantly, cool air flowed through my hood.

The Drexian hooked a blaster on the waistband of my suit without asking me if I knew how to shoot it, then he slipped strange mitts over my hands, tugging them hard. It felt a bit like I was a doll being dressed up, but I tried not to take offense. I doubted the Drexian had ever been sent out on a mission with someone like me before or anyone who wasn't a Drexian warrior.

"These suction hands will keep us from falling off the hull," he said matter of factly before flipping up his own hood and initiating the oxygen then pulling on identical mitts.

I twisted my hands, checking out the black mitts that

looked more like sturdy oven gloves than cool, alien tech. "Got it."

The Drexian leveled a serious gaze at me. "Once we're inside, stay behind me. The suits have comms links within them, so if we get separated, tap your wristband until you get a signal."

Since my plan was to access the ship's brig through the vents, I was planning to get separated. I gave him a thumbs up, my pulse fluttering as the pilot activated an energy field that separated the front half of the ship from us.

When a side hatch spiraled open, I drew in a sharp breath. Even though I was wearing an environmental suit, I could feel a hint of the frigid air as I followed the Drexian outside the ship. I mimicked his movements precisely, flattening my hands against the hull of the Kronock ship.

"Don't look down," I whispered to myself, as we moved across one scale-like hull panel and then another. The Drexian ship was to the side, but there was nothing below my feet but empty space.

"Just like scaling a house," I told myself even though I rarely scaled the sides of houses anymore, preferring to pull off my heists when I was invited to house parties, or to avoid them altogether by entering through the ground floor of a mansion. Still, my early days had involved scaling walls and clambering down roofs, and I tried to convince myself that this was nothing more than that. "Except falling here means I never land."

I gave my head a small shake, reminding myself that this was all a mental game, and I needed to focus. If I concentrated on the job at hand, I wouldn't fall, and I wouldn't fail. I never did. Well, almost never.

I drew in a deep breath, glad for the cool flow of oxygen, and my heartbeat steadied. Ahead of me, the Drexian paused on the hull. I stopped as well, waiting for the metal chute to open. We didn't have to wait long, the flap rising, and a collection of scrap metal spiraled out. After a beat during which I was sure he was determining if there was any more trash to be dumped, the Drexian ducked inside, and I followed as quickly as possible and right before the metal flap clanged shut behind me.

The inside of the trash chute was surprisingly large, and we could both stand with easy clearance for our heads. Now that we weren't having to use our special gloves to stay attached to the ship, we moved faster, jogging down the circular tube.

When we got to the far end, there was a round covering like the one that opened to the outside, but this one opened to the inside of the ship. The Drexian glanced back at me before taking his blaster off his waist and throwing a shoulder at the barrier.

It flew open, and he leapt into the ship, sweeping his blaster arm wide as he scanned the interior. "Clear," he called back to me.

I jumped from the chute, joining him in the industrial room that featured grimy metal walls and scraped up floors. There was no sign of any of the aliens, which made me breathe a sigh of relief. The longer I could go without laying eyes on one, the better.

I thought back to what I'd memorized about the ship layout combined with what Vox had told me. "The trash chutes are located near the bottom of the battleship, not too far from the brig."

"If Jaxon is in the brig," The Drexian muttered darkly, giving voice to what we both feared.

"If he's anywhere, he's probably there," I said, moving toward the door behind the security officer. "Even if they interrogate him, Vox said that's usually not far from the cells."

The Drexian didn't respond, but I noticed him flinch.

We stepped outside the room, but before I could say that we needed to go left, something huge and gray flashed in front of me, taking the Drexian officer down before I could scream, or he could fire his blaster.

CHAPTER
SEVEN

Jaxon

The wailing woke me from a fitful sleep, and I jolted up, wondering if I'd been the one emitting the noise before realizing that it was coming from somewhere deep within the Kronock battleship. I brushed my hands quickly over my body—a reflexive habit after having creatures scurrying across me while I slept—and stood, as a faint red light flashed at the end of the corridor.

"Kalex," I said, curling my hands into fists by my sides. If the Kronock alarms were sounding, it was because they were under attack from the Drexians. Kalex and Vekron had come for me, and it was only a matter of time before Kronock blood filled the battleship, and the air hummed with the sound of their agonizing screams.

Elation surged through me, as well as a healthy dose of

vengeance. As soon as I got out, I was going to show the Kronock what happened when they went up against the Drexians. Correction. When they went up against Inferno Force.

I paced the length of my cramped cell, my bare feet slapping on the hard floor. Now that I knew the battle had begun, my body tingled with anticipation and the desire to fight. It had been too long since I'd blasted a Kronock, and my fingers buzzed with the thought of gripping a weapon.

Blades, I thought. *I hope my Drexian brothers bring blades with them.*

I wouldn't mind blasting our enemy, but after being tortured by them, I welcomed the chance to spill blood the way our ancestors did, slashing their arched blades in ancient battle.

The alarms grew louder and guttural Kronock voices spilled down the hall that held my cell, even though no warriors had yet appeared.

"Patience," I told myself. I'd boarded enough ships to know how long it took to search a battleship, especially if enemy fighters were attempting to repulse the Drexian incursion, which I knew they would.

The Kronock were nothing, if not fierce and relentless. They wouldn't let their ship fall without a vicious fight. I strode to the iron bars and clenched them between my fingers. If only I could get out and join the battle.

Then I glanced down at myself. Even in the dim shadows, my bare torso was mottled with bruises that ranged from vivid purple to a sickly shade of yellow, and those were layered with cuts that oozed blood. My flight suit had been ripped from my body, and I'd been left to shiver in my snug underwear. But even that small amount of fabric was stained with grime and blood.

I didn't look like a valiant warrior ready to take on the Kronock, but that didn't mean my heart didn't remain strong. I hadn't succumbed to the Kronock interrogations, and I hadn't given up hope. I'd known this moment would come.

I squeezed the bars as a door at the end of the corridor flew open, bracing myself for the onslaught of Drexian fighters to pour through. But only a single Kronock stepped into the hallway—the same one who'd dragged me to the interrogation room. His beady eyes narrowed as he stared down the length of the dim corridor, and the flashing red light from outside the hall illuminated his bald, scaly head.

It wasn't smart for me to engage with the enemy, but I couldn't help myself. "Anything wrong out there, friend?"

The hulking alien sneered at me, his thin top lip curling up to reveal sharp teeth.

"If you need some help, you just have to ask." I kept my voice as jovial and light as I had since I'd been brought onto the ship, mostly because it seemed to annoy the Kronock guard.

"We don't need anything from a Drexian," he snarled.

I shrugged, trying to look and sound nonchalant as a row of Kronock pounded past the guard. "You sure? Your friends seem to be in a big hurry."

He flinched visibly, letting loose a growl that filled the hallway between us. "They're eager to kill more Drexians."

The confirmation that my brothers in arms were on the ship make my heart hammer in my chest. "The battle has begun?"

The Kronock tilted his long face at me. "Battle?" Then he let out what I assumed was his version of a laugh, a jagged gurgling noise that made him sound like he was being strangled underwater. "There is no battle."

I fought back my impatience, reminding myself that the Kronock frequently lied. This guard probably wouldn't tell me if the entire ship was being burned down by Drexian firepower. But then doubt niggled at the back of my brain. Why wasn't the Kronock ship trembling from the impact of laser fire? Why didn't I hear screams and blasters?

The guard stepped out for a moment before moving fully inside the corridor, his thick clawed feet scraping on the floor as he lumbered toward me. The hallway remained bathed in shadows, but I could see that there was something behind him. "No one is coming to save you, Drexian."

I steeled myself against his words. No, his lies. The Kronock spewed nothing but lies and hatred, and this low-level guard who'd been tasked with transporting their one Drexian captive was no different. "Then why the alarms?"

He twisted his head for a beat, glancing back to the muffled glow of red flashing outside the corridor. "It was nothing."

More lies. Ship wide alarms did not go off for nothing. I peered through the darkness to see past the thick tail that swung behind him. Was there something aside from his tail being dragged along in the creature's wake? There wasn't enough light to make out much of anything aside from gray scales and hulking limbs, but the shadows were all wrong.

When he reached my cell, he held out a blaster, aiming it squarely at my chest. "Back against the wall, Drexian."

I hesitated, but then decided I didn't want to die when I

was so close to being rescued. I held up my hands as I backed up, but my mind raced. If they were taking me out, that meant they were afraid the enemy was coming for me. I couldn't let myself be taken somewhere my Drexian brothers wouldn't be able to access. And I didn't want to be shoved out an airlock because the Kronock would rather kill me than have me rescued.

Despite holding my hands up in surrender, I stood poised to run as soon as the cell was opened. I'd have a few seconds at most when the guard was busy with the latch, and that would be when I'd make my move.

My heart thumped in my chest as I waited for the door to swing open so I could make a dash for it, but before I could move, the Kronock had thrown something bulky into my cell. I stared down in shock as the door to my cell clanged shut again.

"Thought you'd like a roommate," the guard said with another cruel laugh as he stomped out, leaving me alone with the dead body of a Drexian warrior.

CHAPTER
EIGHT

Samaira

"It's going to be okay," I whispered to myself, as I huddled in the cramped ventilation shaft.

But was it? My hands still shook from the shock of watching the Drexian security officer being taken out by an alien so huge and monstrous I still wasn't sure if I'd imagined it. It had happened so quickly, I hadn't had time to react. My first instinct had been to jump back and when I'd gathered my wits about me to grab my blaster, the Kronock had been standing over the Drexian's unmoving body.

I'd managed not to scream or cry out but had instead crept back into the room with the trash chute and spotted a grate for a ventilation shaft in the wall. The Kronock who'd killed the Drexian had been too busy bellowing about his kill and putting the ship on high alert to hear me, which had been a good thing, since my hands had trembled so hard I'd barely gotten the grate off and myself inside before aliens were coming into the room.

I glanced down at my hands. The trembling had lessened but hadn't completely gone. I clasped them together and took a deep breath. I'd never let a job make me so flustered, but I'd also never seen someone slaughtered in front of my eyes so brutally.

The Drexian had been talking to me seconds before he'd been killed. He'd gotten me into my environmental suit and told me how to use it. He'd kept me behind him so he could lead the way and keep me safe, and he'd paid for it with his life.

My stomach churned, and I pressed my lips together as the tang of bile teased the back of my throat. I didn't want to think about seeing the Drexian's throat slashed open by a monster who looked like a mutated crocodile on two legs, but the image would forever be seared in my brain.

Come on, Samaira. You're tougher than this.

As soon as I said the words in my head, I thought about my mother. Now it was memories of her lilting voice that made me push aside my fear. *You're strong, Samaira. Stronger than you know.*

But I hadn't been strong when she'd died. I'd fallen apart. We all had. My father had never found himself again. I'd found myself running with the rough kids in our neighborhood and proving to myself just how tough I was. But I'd never experienced the confidence I'd felt when my mother had looked into my eyes and told me that I was strong. Not even when I'd been pulling off the most complicated heists of my career.

But I needed that strength now.

Closing my eyes, I centered myself and focused on my breathing. I was alone on an alien battleship with no one to help me, and I was the only hope that the Drexian captive had of being rescued. If what I'd heard the Kronock yelling had been right, they hadn't located the ship that brought us, which meant the stealth shielding was still holding.

The alarms had been wailing since the Drexian officer had been killed, but as far as I could determine the Kronock didn't know how he'd gotten on board or that there'd been anyone else with him. Which meant that for now, I had the advantage.

I almost laughed at this since I was bent over in a ventilation shaft. My neck ached from the odd angle and my legs burned from crouching, but I ignored all of that. I was alive, and I was determined to stay that way.

I was also determined to carry out the rescue mission. No way was the Drexian going to die in vain. Not when he'd taken a proverbial bullet for me.

"Okay, Samaira," I said to myself. "Ventilation shafts are your happy place. Let's see where these babies take us, why don't we?"

Doing a quick mental review of the schematics, I got on my hands and knees and started moving quietly through the metal tubing. Luckily for me, the ship was built for enormous aliens, so everything was oversized—including the inner workings of the battleship.

I wasn't used to ventilation shafts being on the floor, but I found that I preferred not moving over the heads of the Kronock, especially after I'd seen what their heads looked like. Not that their feet were any better, but the occasional glimpse of a thick clawed foot was better than seeing their bionic eyes and dinosaur-like jaws.

I counted the turns in my head as well as the distance I'd traveled, moving deeper inside the ship. After a while, the noises of aliens running and barking orders to each other subsided. I paused at a grate leading back into the ship. If I was right—and the schematics and Vox's knowledge had brought me to the right place—I should be in the corridor leading to the ship's brig. And if the Drexian was anywhere, he should be there.

I paused, straining to hear any sounds that would indicate that I was right—or really wrong. It was silent, which was either good news or bad.

Here goes nothing, I thought, as I gingerly unfastened the grate and poked my head out. If I'd thought the ventilation shafts had been dark, the corridor I was peering into wasn't much better with only faint red light glowing from a far door.

I allowed my eyes to adjust for a second then slipped out fully, lowering the grate silently and flattening myself against the wall. The good news? My appearance hadn't provoked the thundering approach of terrifying aliens. The bad news? I didn't see or hear any signs of a Drexian.

Squinting down the dim hallway, I could make out rows of cells fronted by iron bars. I'd expected something more techy from an alien battleship, but after seeing the brutes who occupied it, maybe I'd been expecting too much. Primitive bars were fitting for a species that appeared to be as brutal as the Kronock.

I moved on tiptoes down the length of the hallway, keeping my back against the wall. If the Drexian wasn't here,

I'd just sneak back into the vent shaft, crawl back to the trash chute, and make my way back out to the Drexian ship. I was mentally prepared to do just that when I heard a sound at the end of the cells.

I stopped walking, one foot hovering in mid-air as I held my breath and listened again. Had I heard someone breathing or was I hallucinating? I wouldn't have been surprised if I was hearing things that weren't there.

Just as I was about to pivot and head back to the opening into the vent shaft, I heard it again. A breath.

"You aren't one of them." The voice that emerged from the darkness was low and calm, nothing like the rough, rasping language of the aliens.

"Neither are you," I replied, my pulse quickening when I realized that I'd located the Drexian prisoner after all. "Are you Jaxon?"

There was a heavy pause. "Who are you?"

Was this guy really going to ask me for ID when I was here to break him out? "I'm Sam. The Drexians sent me."

"You aren't Drexian." That wasn't a question, and he sounded defeated as he said it. "Then what are you? A Gredarian mercenary?"

"Human." I glanced back at the door at the far end of the hallway, wondering how much time we had until the aliens appeared to check on their prisoner. I continued down the corridor, not bothering to tiptoe. When I reached the Drexian's cell, I peered through the bars, inhaling sharply and trying not to physically recoil from the stench.

Even though he was mostly in shadows, I could make out a nearly naked Drexian sitting on a metal bench with his elbow on his knees and his shoulders hunched over. In front of him lay the crumpled body of the Drexian officer who'd been assigned to me—the one who'd died in front of my eyes.

"How did...?" My words trailed, my mouth dry as I tried to pull my gaze from the dead Drexian with blood pooling around his head.

"Was he with you?"

I nodded.

Even though he barely glanced up at me, the Drexian sighed. "How many more are there?"

"Just me."

His head snapped up faster than I would have thought possible. "Just you?" He groaned. "My only hope of getting away from this hell pit is a human female?"

I bristled at the scorn dripping from his words. "Yeah, it is. And I'm getting less inclined to save your ass by the second."

We glared at each other through the bars until a jangling sound at the end of the corridor made us both look away.

Bloody hell. Time was up.

CHAPTER
NINE

Jaxon

My body tensed as a clanging noise came from the end of the corridor. I cut my eyes to the noise then back to the woman standing outside my cell. I still hadn't determined why she was there, or how she'd managed to get past the Kronock, but the last thing I needed to deal with was a female. Especially a human one.

She glanced back as well, then her gaze darted toward the floor and her hand went to a blaster hooked to her waistband.

"You should go," I said, sensing her desire to flee. I hadn't seen where she'd emerged from, but I suspected she could still get back if she moved quickly.

She met my eyes and shook her head, although when the noise outside the far door passed, her shoulders sagged with obvious relief.

"If they catch you, you might not be as lucky as this guy," I said.

Her eyes lowered to the Drexian on the floor, her full lips tightening into a thin line. "My mission is to get you out. He died guarding me. I'm not going to let his sacrifice be wasted."

An honorable sentiment, but a foolish one, considering that we were inside a Kronock battleship, and I was locked behind iron bars. I gave my head a shake, still processing the unbelievable fact that my rescuer was a female. Not only that, a human female who didn't look scarier or bigger than any other woman from their planet I'd ever seen.

I eyed the choppy layers of brown hair that reached her jawline and dark eyes flashing at me in challenge. She didn't look especially girly, although she was the type of female who would have turned heads even if she didn't try. Her wide eyes, heavily fringed with lashes, and full lips made her impossible not to notice. Unfortunately, the Drexian environmental suit made the rest of her body blend into the grimy walls, so I couldn't tell if she was slim or curvy, but she looked about average height for a human woman, which still made her significantly smaller than me. The Kronock would dwarf her.

"You ready?"

I pulled my gaze back to her face as she moved to the bars, running her fingers along them. "Ready?"

"Like I said, I'm here to get you out. You ready to go?"

I fought the urge to bark out a laugh. It was so ludicrous that I wondered if I was hallucinating. Or maybe it was a trap by the Kronock. "They really sent you and not a fleet of warriors?"

"Captain Kalex wanted to get you out with as few losses as possible and without tipping off your enemy." She kept her gaze away from the dead Drexian, but she swallowed hard. "That's why he brought me in."

This was Kalex's idea? I frowned. Kalex was Inferno Force. We fought hard and took chances, risking our lives on impulsive and dangerous missions all the time. And now he was sending in a woman? "What made him think you were a better choice than an Inferno Force warrior?"

She jiggled the heavy metal lock keeping the cell impenetrable, standing back as she swung open the door. "Because I can do things like that."

I dropped my gaze to the open door, the lock dangling off it. I'd shaken the bars until I was sure they'd rip from the floor, pulling so hard my hands had gone raw, but within a few seconds she'd opened my cell—and without any visible key. "You're with intelligence?"

"Now I am. MI-6."

I stared at her. Were those letters and number supposed to mean anything to me?

"British secret service," she added, stepping into the cell with me. "I guess they aren't as big a deal outside of Earth, but they're one of the top intelligence agencies in the world."

"They? I thought you said you were part of them."

"Right. I am." She crouched down beside the crumpled Drexian, resting a hand on his shoulder. "I just keep forgetting. I haven't been with them long. To be honest, I was on the other side of the law for a long time. It's hard to get used to being one of the good guys. Official good guys, that is."

I knew my brain had been muddled from the sleep deprivation and torture, but the woman wasn't making any sense. "What do you mean you were on the other side?"

She sighed, glancing impatiently behind her, as she started to unfasten the Drexian warrior's environmental suit "I was a thief, okay?" She waved a hand at the cell. "How do you think I got that open so fast? They don't teach you my kind of skills in MI-6. At least I don't think they do."

The feeling of irritation that I was being rescued by a woman was now compounded by a sense of dread. Not only was she a human female—she was a criminal. A criminal who was undressing a fallen Drexian hero.

"What are you doing?" I snapped.

She peered up at me, swiping her hair from her face. "Don't get me wrong, you look great in your skivvies, but since I plan to sneak you from the ship unseen, it would help a lot of you could be in one of these invisible suits."

My face warmed as it struck me for the first time that I was standing in front of her in little more than a scrap of black fabric that barely covered my crotch.

She glanced down at the Drexian, patting his arm. "I don't think he'll mind."

That was actually a good strategy, and she was right. If the Drexian had come on this mission to save me, he would have gladly given up his environmental suit if it upped the odds I'd make it out alive. I bent over and helped her tug the suit off his heavy body, saying a silent thanks to my Drexian brother for giving his life for me.

Once we'd stripped the Drexian down to his standard issue uniform, she pushed the pile of shimmery fabric at me. "I hate to rush this, but we should really crack on if we want to get you off this ship."

As much as I didn't like being bossed around by a woman, I couldn't argue with her logic. The Kronock might not monitor me frequently, but I didn't want to take any chances. When I'd gotten into the suit, I tapped the wrist cuff to shrink it to me. Not only did I blend into the walls, but I was also no longer shivering from the cold.

"Right," the woman said, spinning on her heel. "Follow me and try not to make any noise."

I didn't move as she strode from the cell. "What about him?"

She turned and followed my gaze to the Drexian on the floor. "Listen, mate. I'm gutted that he didn't make it, but do you really plan to drag him through the ventilation shafts with us?"

We were getting out through the vent shafts? That was a new one. I wasn't used to sneaking around enemy ships, although I had to give the woman credit for reaching me without getting caught. Maybe I should follow her lead in getting out. "If that's how we're going, then yeah, I do. I'm not leaving him behind for the Kronock to experiment on— or worse."

Something flickered across her face, and she gave me a curt nod. "Fine, but you're going to have to drag him, big guy." She held up a finger. "And I don't want to hear a word of complaint that it's taking too long. Vents don't always go in a straight line."

"Fine." I hooked my hands under the Drexian warrior's armpits, flinching from the pain of exertion and sliding him behind me as I followed her from the cell and down the hall, careful not to leave a blood trail on the floor.

I shouldn't have been surprised that the woman was so

irritating. From my limited experience with women from Earth, they were too independent. I only had to look at Kalex and how he fought endlessly with the space station astro-architect to be reminded that human women were not for me. My own foolish yearning to be matched with one had been knocked from me long ago.

Unwanted memories rushed over me, the sharp sting of pain overwhelming the discomfort of moving and pulling the Drexian with me. I grunted and forced thoughts of the human who rejected me from my mind as I watched Sam open the grate covering the vent shaft, her slender neck bent forward and her hair spilling over her face. An unwanted flutter of desire stirred in my gut, and I frowned at my weakness. It didn't matter how alluring women might look, experience had taught me they were nothing but trouble.

I averted my eyes as she crawled into the metal tube, glad that the environmental suit made her curves just a shimmering outline. Tugging the body behind me, I followed her inside the wall, hunching over so that I was almost on my belly.

"How far do we have to go?" I asked once the vent cover was replaced, and darkness enveloped us.

A deep sigh was her only response. I bit back a sharp comment about how much faster it would be to battle our way through the ship. "Forget I said anything."

"I already have," she said, her soft voice echoing back as she started to crawl forward.

Grekking woman.

CHAPTER
TEN

Samaira

I cast a quick look over my shoulder. I could hear Jaxon behind me as he crawled through the vent, dragging the dead Drexian behind him, but all I could make out in the dark was the occasional flash of his eyes.

I didn't ask if he was okay. Not only did I not want to make any noise as we crept through the ship, but I also didn't want the git to think I was worried about him. I was still annoyed by the lukewarm reception he'd given me, and the skeptical way he'd eyed me when I'd told him I'd come to rescue his sorry arse.

I rolled my eyes, even though no one could see my expression of annoyance. Did he really think he was the first bloke to size me up and think I couldn't cut it because I was a woman? I knew the Drexians were used to being the big, tough aliens in charge, but I hadn't been fully briefed on what male chauvinist pigs they were.

"Big, bloody surprise," I murmured to myself, before remembering that I was trying to stay silent.

All I'd heard since the Big Reveal was how hot the Drexians were, and how they'd been protecting Earth for decades. They were massive, muscular warriors who believed in honor and loyalty and would fight to the death to protect their species—and apparently ours.

If you asked me, it had all sounded too good to be true. Then we'd learned that they'd been secretly—well, aside from a few in-the-know government agencies—taking human women as mates. But people weren't upset. As a matter of fact, women had fallen all over themselves to become one of the tribute brides for the Drexians.

They could have them, I thought. The Drexians weren't anything special. Not if Jaxon was anything to go by.

My mind drifted back to the sight of him in nothing but snug boxer briefs, his sizable package impossible to miss along with his washboard abs and massive chest muscles. Okay, so he was hot. That didn't mean he wasn't a sexist prat.

I slid my knees across the steel floor of the vent, forcing myself not to think about the Drexian and to focus instead on taking slow even breaths, despite the heat that sent sweat trickling down my temples. It had been a while since I'd crawled through a vent shaft this long, and I'd forgotten how my knees ached from the constant pressure.

Behind me, Jaxon's breathing was heavy, which made sense. He was lugging dead weight behind him. Although my strategic side thought bringing the dead Drexian had been a mistake, I had to admire Jaxon for insisting on it. I wouldn't want to be left behind for the scaly aliens to abuse or experiment on either.

I'd been counting turns in my head, so after a few more meters, I slowed and ran my fingers along the grate. "This should be it."

"Should be?" Jaxon's voice was a low rasp, but it conveyed plenty of doubt.

I wished it wasn't so dark so I could shoot him a murderous look. "This *is* it."

Listening for evidence that one of the aliens was inside the room with the waste disposal chute, I held my breath. Without me asking, Jaxon did the same.

"We should be clear," I whispered, working the grate cover swiftly and propping it open as I slid out. When my feet hit the floor, I held the grate open for Jaxon, who managed to squeeze through the opening and pull the Drexian behind him.

He scanned the compact space. "Where are we?"

"This is where the Kronock toss out their space trash. The Drexian ship is attached to the hull of the battleship right next to the chute's flap."

Jaxon raised an eyebrow but nodded. "So, we crawl out the chute and hope the Kronock don't decide to toss anything before we make it outside?"

"Pretty much." I tugged on the suction mitts I'd jammed into the pockets of the environmental suit, and Jaxon followed my lead, finding identical gloves in his own pockets. We both flipped up our hoods and closed them over our faces.

Jaxon hoisted the dead Drexian over one shoulder and

headed for the metal opening of the chute, propping it open for me. "See you on the other side, Sam."

At least he called me by my name. I clamored up into the chute, my heart racing as I shuffled down the length of the large tube. It wasn't every day that I left the climate-and-gravity-controlled inside of a battleship to go into space.

Even though I'd done this once before, the Drexian officer had been leading the way the first time. Now, I was going first. I only hoped I didn't slip or overshoot the ship. The thought of clinging to the outside of an alien battleship for any longer than absolutely necessary was terrifying.

Though the noise was muffled, I heard Jaxon entering the chute behind me. Once he'd made his way through and was right behind me, I leaned on the flap leading outside, keeping one hand fully suctioned to the inside of the chute.

The steel covering lifted, revealing the gaping blackness beyond. With a shuddering breath, I forced myself to twist and plant a hand on the hull. Pulling myself fully outside, I moved hand over hand across the gray scales of the battleship.

Don't look down, I reminded myself. Do not look down.

Jaxon was moving slowly beside me, his progress slowed by the body draped over his back. Still, he seemed to keep up with me easily.

Before I could be annoyed that the injured Drexian could move just as fast as me even with the added weight of an extra body, my hand hit something hard.

The Drexian ship. I almost cheered. We'd made it back. I pounded my hand hard against the invisible hull, and the circular hatch spiraled open, revealing the inside of the ship.

The pilot was behind the energy field, but he'd twisted in his seat, a relieved expression on his face.

I climbed inside, stumbling to the side so Jaxon could follow me.

"I was starting to think you might not..." the pilot started to say, before Jaxon entered and placed the dead warrior on the floor.

"The Kronock got him," Jaxon said before I could offer an explanation.

The pilot nodded grimly. "He knew the risks going in."

I hadn't been emotional when I'd been inside the Kronock ship but being back in the relative safety of the Drexian ship made a lump form in my throat. I'd only had one job in the past go so wrong someone had died, and like back then, I couldn't help feeling responsible. Suddenly, I was back on Earth staring at the dead body of my friend, my ears ringing, and the scream trapped in my throat.

I sank into one of the seats as the hatch closed and the energy field was disabled, my entire body shaking. Jaxon opened an inset cabinet and found a pair of boots, slipping them on his bare, bruised feet before he sat across from me. He pushed back his hood and ran a hand through his long hair. When he finally looked up, his brow furrowed. "You okay?"

I managed a weak nod, but I couldn't manage to unfasten my hood. My arms wouldn't move.

Jaxon reached over and pulled it off for me. "It's okay. We made it." He eyed me as he strapped me into the seat, tugging on the restraints.

I concentrated on taking long steady breaths until the

ringing in my ears faded and my heart stopped racing. Nice going, Sam, I thought. *You pulled off the most difficult heist of your career and then you have a panic attack.* I averted my eyes from Jaxon as he took his seat and strapped himself in.

"We haven't made it yet," the pilot said. "We still have to get through the energy rift, whenever the next one appears."

"How long will that be?" Jaxon asked.

"I've been timing them since I've been sitting out here. They aren't at regular intervals, but I don't think we'll have to wait long." He swiped his fingers across the shiny console that stretched in front of him. "Unless you two object, I'm going to move us off the Kronock ship and position us near where the rift usually appears."

"No objections here," Jaxon said. "The farther away from that ship the better."

The Drexian ship disengaged with a slight jerk, moving away from the hulking battleship and pivoting to face the opposite direction.

I released a tentative breath, grateful not to be looking at the mammoth monstrosity of a ship and be reminded of the creatures inside. Then I jerked forward, the safety straps keeping me from flying across the ship and into Jaxon's lap.

"What the *grek*?" Jaxon gasped, as the ship spun wildly, alerts sounding and lights flashing.

"It seems we were hit by space trash," the pilot yelled, over the cacophony of beeps.

"Did it do serious damage?" Jaxon called back.

The pilot let out a series of curses I couldn't understand. "It knocked out our stealth shielding."

My stomach lurched as a swarm of alien fighter ships emerged in front of us. "Bloody hell."

Jaxon leaned forward, his face ashen as he stared out the front of the ship. "Bloody *grekking* hell."

CHAPTER
ELEVEN

Jaxon

"Can we outrun them?" Sam asked, her voice shrill above the frantic sounds of the pilot cursing in Drexian and the ship beeping.

I eyed the gunmetal-gray fighters swarming from the side of the battleship. "Not all of them." I unhooked my safety straps and jumped from my seat, plopping down in the co-pilot's seat and fastening myself into that. Although my body still ached, the adrenaline and my desire to escape masked any pain. "Any sign of that energy rift?"

The pilot gave me a grateful look but shook his head. "Not yet. Even if it does appear, I don't know if we can reach it." He inclined his head toward the incoming enemy ships. "It usually appears at coordinates on the other side of all them."

I gulped, cutting my eyes to the familiar console. Our engine was still functional, but the port side of the ship had been hit with whatever space trash had come from the chute. That impact had damaged the stealth shielding and caused a slow fuel leak. Even if the Kronock weren't on an intercept course, we wouldn't be able to wait them out. "We need to outrun them."

The pilot spared me a quick glance. "But where are we running to?"

"Doesn't matter. We need to keep them from blowing us to bits long enough for that rift to appear."

"You think they'll try to blow us up?" the human asked from behind me.

Incoming laser fire that exploded to one side of us was her answer.

"This might be your first experience with the Kronock," I told her, "but it isn't ours. And I'd rather they blow us up than take us captive."

I was not going back into that battleship, I promised myself. Not if it meant dying from slow torture. I'd rather die out here in blazing glory.

Our ship dipped low, skirting beneath a pair of incoming fighters and spinning as we came up behind them. The pilot let loose with a spray of laser fire, which hit one of the enemy ship's wings. It spiraled off and crashed into the hull of the battleship.

"Nice shooting," I said.

"Why don't you take over monitoring for the energy rift while I hold off the attack?"

My pulse quickened as I focused on the console again, my

gaze locking on the energy readings. No fluctuations yet, but I could see where the pilot had been tracking them, and I could see the regular intervals he'd mentioned.

The ship lurched to one side and more explosions illuminated the cockpit, but I kept my focus on the readouts. I did not want to miss the appearance of the rift and our chance to get back to Drexian space. At least the heat of the battle kept me from thinking about my injuries.

Since Sam had found me, I'd barely had a moment to dwell on my aching ribs or the bruises covering my body. Even the open wounds didn't bother me now that I was away from the fetid cell and not shivering from the numbing cold.

"Brace!" The pilot screamed as he banked hard to one side.

The safety straps caught me before I slammed into the wall of the ship, and I sucked in a sharp breath from the pain. So much for not thinking about my injuries.

Peering up through the glass, my mouth fell open. We appeared to be flying through a web of Kronock fighters, and I was amazed that none of their laser fire was hitting us. Our pilot was weaving and spinning masterfully, managing to draw enemy fire and then dodging at the last moment so it actually hit one of their own ships. He was depleting their forces with their own weapons fire.

"You sure you aren't Inferno Force?" I asked him as he stopped the ship and flipped it upside down to fire at a Kronock fighter below us.

"Not yet." He gave me a wild grin, clearly in his element as he flew and fired. "It's a dream of mine to join."

"You've got my recommendation," I said, as we soared above a row of advancing ships. Glancing back, I saw that we'd left the battleship behind us, drawing the enemy fighters and scattering them as we cut a wide arc through space.

"Thanks! Any sign of the rift?"

I tore my gaze away from the battle and looked at the readouts. "Still nothing." I squinted at the numbers. "I *am* getting energy signatures from a nearby planet."

"A planet? Maybe I can use that as further distraction and to disperse the fighters."

I gave him the coordinates. "You think we should fly away from where we expect the energy rift to appear? We *are* losing fuel."

"I need to keep us in one piece until then, and I'm not sure my fancy flying will do that for much longer."

I didn't want to argue with him since he was the pilot, and he'd risked his life to rescue me, but the thought of missing the energy rift made my gut tighten. "It looks like there are a couple of smaller moons orbiting the planet."

"I'll take the Kronock around them. I should be able to lose some of the weaker flyers that way."

I chanced a glance over my shoulder at Sam. She had her eyes closed and her hands gripped tightly around her knees. Her light brown skin looked tinged with green, and her lips were a tight white line. "You okay back there?"

She didn't respond.

"Sam!" I yelled.

She twitched and her eyes flew open. "What? Did we go through the rift yet?"

"I just wanted to make sure you were okay."

"I'm fine," she snapped. "Just wondering why you don't equip these ships with barf bags."

I stifled a grin and turned back to my console. "Not much longer. Isn't that what you said when we were going through the vent?"

She muttered something that sounded like an invitation to bite her, but I must have heard wrong. Then again, I'd learned from the Gatazoid wedding planner Serge that human expressions often made no sense.

A blue line flashed on my console, and my heart raced. "The energy rift is opening!"

"Punching in coordinates," the pilot said. "I'll whip around this moon and take us into it."

The moon we were fast approaching was covered in white swirls, although the planet behind it looked significantly larger and more populated. Even from a distance, I noticed entire swaths of land illuminated and gray clouds swirling over massive oceans. I'd never seen an actual Kronock planet before—only other species' planets that the Kronock had colonized or obliterated—but this planet was deep enough in Kronock space that it must have been one of the planets populated by their kind. My stomach churned at the thought of so many of our enemy living peacefully while their armies invaded other worlds.

Then we were skirting around the moon and the planet disappeared from view. I couldn't think about anything but getting back to Drexian space, I reminded myself. Then I could tell Kalex everything I'd learned and devise a plan to come back with enough of a force to take them out.

As we rounded the moon, I spotted the ripple in space. The pilot's plan had worked. He'd drawn the Kronock ships away from the battleship and the opening rift, and we had a clear shot to it. I could almost see the Island in front of us, the clear hull glittering in the darkness of space, and the glowing inclinator tubes twisting and spiraling inside. It wasn't home, but I ached to see it, nonetheless.

"I'm giving it everything we've got left," the pilot said, swiping his fingers across the console.

I waited for the ship to burst forward and to be pushed back against my seat, but that never came. Instead, the ship shuddered as a blast impacted us from the back.

"We're hit!" Sam screamed.

Alarms sounded as we were flipped upside down, the ship spinning aimlessly. I tried to reach the console, but we were moving so fast it was hard to control my arms. Were we still heading toward the rift? I desperately attempted to peer out the front of the ship, but everything was a blur as we continued to spiral.

I was aware of the pilot's arms also flailing, but he was finally able to reach his console. The ship straightened out, although we were no longer hurtling through space. We were racing toward the surface of the moon we'd been passing. We dropped below the white swirls, descending quickly into the atmosphere, but all I could see was blackness. From the images swirling past the glass, it appeared that the moon was enveloped in darkness.

"I can only slow our descent," the pilot said, his voice agonized. "I can't stop it."

I cast a final look back at Sam, whose brown eyes were wide and filled with fear. "Brace for impact!"

Then we hit the tip of a sharp, obsidian mountain peak, the impact flipping us over and hurtling us toward the ground. Our fall was slowed by an inky web of vines that reached long tendrils around our hull as we crashed through them. The female's screams were the last thing I heard before the blackness became absolute, and everything went quiet.

CHAPTER
TWELVE

Samaira

I lifted my head, the pain in my neck making me wince. The ship's alarms had stopped sounding, and instead of the scraping of metal as our hull had plummeted through the dense jungle, there was silence.

"Is everyone okay?" Jaxon's voice was a croak, but it was comforting to hear something that told me I wasn't alone.

Opening my eyes, I could tell that the ship had landed on its side. The safety straps were the only things keeping me from falling, the stiff fabric cutting into my shoulders. "I'm okay."

I swiveled my head to see Jaxon shaking the pilot's arm. The arm that wasn't pinned to the seat by the tree branch that had crashed through the front glass of the ship and impaled the Drexian's left side. Even from my vantage point, I could tell the pilot was dead from the way his head lolled to one side, and his arms dangled like he was a puppet who'd had his strings cut.

"*Grek*." Jaxon unhooked himself from the copilot's chair and pulled himself up so he could feel for a pulse on the other Drexian's neck. After a few moments, his shoulders sagged in defeat.

A wave of sadness engulfed me. Now I'd lost both members of the team who'd come with me on this mission. This was exactly why I hated working on teams. Losing people was too hard. It was better to go it alone and only risk yourself.

Jaxon reached over and closed the pilot's eyes, pressing his own together for a beat. "He was a Drexian warrior, and he died on a mission and battling against the Kronock. He died an honorable death."

I wasn't sure if I was fully onboard with the Drexian's code of honor—I was a thief, after all—but I was glad it made Jaxon feel better. "He was a good pilot."

Jaxon nodded. "When we get back, I'll recommend both Drexians for commendations."

I glanced back at the other dead Drexian, who'd rolled across the floor so that he was pressed up against the seat opposite me. "I like your confidence."

"What do you mean?"

I met the Drexian's eyes then waved a hand over my head at the mangled ship. The jet-black interior was covered in scrapes and dents, wiring hanging down from a panel overhead. Steam came from the front of the ship, and the scent of char permeated the cockpit. "Look at us. We're in a spaceship that's been destroyed. The other two members of our team are dead, and you're clearly injured. I'm impressed that you assume we're going to make it back to Drexian space."

He looked at me like I was the crazy one. "Of course, we're going to make it back. We've just had a few setbacks."

"Setbacks?"

He ignored my incredulous question, instead, peering out the front of the ship to the dark and dense moon beyond. If the willowy, black tree trunk jutting through our window was any indication, we were in a thick forest of some kind, although the air coming through was hot and humid enough to make me think it was more like a rainforest. A very dark rainforest, through which little light permeated.

"We know the air is breathable," he said. "That's one thing going for us."

I stopped breathing as soon as he said that. I'd been inhaling the air on an alien moon without even thinking about it. I was lucky it wasn't poisonous. "Are we sure?"

He flicked his gaze at me, his lips quirking up at the corners. "It's denser than a human is probably used to, but it's breathable. Otherwise, we'd both be dead already."

I resumed breathing, noticing that the air did feel soupier. "What is this place?"

Jaxon peered down at the console that was blinking erratically and flashing numbers and symbols and random intervals. "All I know for sure is that it's one of the moons of the Kronock planet. The planet itself looked inhabited and technologically developed. I don't think we can say the same about this place."

I peered out the shattered glass, shivering at the sight of dark foliage and trees so black it looked like they'd been scorched. "I guess that's a good thing. If we'd crashed on a planet inhabited by your enemy, we'd be as good as dead."

"If we were lucky," Jaxon grumbled as he tapped the console.

I fiddled with the latch of my safety strap, but it was stuck, so I jerked hard at it. As much fun as it was to hang sideways, I was ready to free myself.

With a sigh, Jaxon made his way to me, pushing my hands aside. "Let me do it."

I glowered at him, but he was too focused on working on my straps to notice. After about a minute, I said. "Having trouble there, big guy?"

"It's stuck. The crash damaged the latch. I'll need to cut you out." He reached overhead to where a curved blade was fastened to the ceiling behind black netting and freed it. Then he positioned himself between me and the hull and started cutting.

"I think you should—" I said when I realized where he was standing, but it was too late.

When he sawed through the strap, it gave way, and I fell right on top on him. The two of us rolled to the side and ended up with him lying flat on top of me.

Jaxon's eyes were wide, and his face was so close to me that his breath mingled with mine. Gravity and the strange angle of the ship had pinned us both between the back of a seat and the wall. "Sorry, I didn't mean to..."

"It's okay," I said, trying not to pay attention to the firmness of his muscles pressed against me. "I think you need to slip your hand behind my waist for leverage."

His brow furrowed but he nodded, tentatively sliding one

hand down my body and around my back. Once his arm was around me, my body was arched even closer to his for a beat. His breath caught in his chest and his pupils darkened, his gaze drifting to my lips before he grunted and heaved himself off me.

I clambered to my feet, brushing off my environmental suit and smoothing my hair. "Thanks."

He didn't respond, instead giving me another grunt and turning away. "We can't stay here."

I glanced outside the ship and saw nothing but gnarled, ebony trees and light barely sneaking through to the undergrowth. "Why not? It doesn't look so great out there. I've never seen a forest that's so black. How do we know it's not been burned to a crisp? It might not be populated by Kronock, but if it's a forest it's populated by something, and I'm not a big nature girl."

Jax waited for me to stop rambling. "The Kronock saw us go down. If their ships didn't follow us down, they will soon. From what I could see on our approach, the place isn't huge so finding one Drexian ship that no longer has stealth shielding won't be hard for them."

I'd forgotten that the ship was no longer invisible, and that the enemy wouldn't give up just because we'd crashed. "At least the ship matches everything outside."

Jax cut his eyes to the dusky surroundings. "I'm not sure if that's a good thing or not."

I shivered at the darkness, thinking I agreed with him. Aside from having breathable air, the moon didn't appear very hospitable. I glanced at each of the dead Drexians in turn. "What do we do with them? I know you can't carry them both."

Jaxon took a deep breath. "We store them in here. When the Drexians rescue us, we can retrieve them."

Again, with the complete confidence that we'd be rescued. I was starting to envy this blind trust. I'd never been able to rely on anyone the way this guy relied on his people. I thought about telling him about the tracking beacon ring Vekron had given me but decided against it. As soon as I activated it, the signal would attract anyone who could detect it, and at the moment, the enemy was still hot on our tail. No chance the Drexians would pick it up and reach us before the Kronock, and from what I'd seen, Kronock captivity did not look like a good time.

Jaxon hacked at the tree impaling the pilot and then unhooked him, dragging his body and placing it next to the other one, each movement making him wince in obvious pain. As I watched, he rooted around in one of the inset cabinets until he found a couple of shiny pouches that he unfurled with a snap of his wrist.

"A body bag?" I gaped as he unzipped one long oval of crinkly fabric. "These ships come supplied with body bags?"

He shrugged, handing me one end and flinching from the movement. "Our missions are dangerous, and we never leave a Drexian behind."

I helped him get the warriors into the bags, panting when we were done maneuvering the bulky bodies. The humid air made sweat trickle down my face and the small of my back, and I unfastened the top of my environmental suit.

"I wouldn't take that off entirely," Jaxon said, as he dug around in another cabinet, filling a pack with more pouches. "We might want to move unseen."

I stopped unfastening it but sighed. Wearing so many

layers in this place was sweltering, and for a moment I was jealous that the Drexian had almost nothing under his environmental suit.

"We might want to take care of your injuries before we head outside," I said, cutting a quick glance at the side he favored and instinctively held an arm over.

"I'm fine," he grumbled.

"I appreciate the tough-guy act, mate, but you'll move faster if we can at least tape your ribs, which from the way you're protecting them, I assume are broken. Frankly, I don't want to have to slow down for you, so it's either let me tape your ribs or make peace with being left in the dust."

He opened his mouth to argue but instead a rough laugh escaped from his lips. He grabbed a pouch from his pack and handed it to me. Unfastening it, I saw that it was a Drexian version of a first aid kit. Way more techy, but it did have something that looked like medical tape.

I unrolled some and eyed his suit, which he rolled down to his waist, revealing a heavily tattooed arm and lots of injuries. I stifled a gasp at the deep bruises marring his flesh, and then carefully wrapped his midsection in tape. The Drexian tape went on like normal medical tape but then it almost appeared to vanish into the skin. I brushed my fingers over it. I could still feel it, but it had melded with the skin and sealed the cuts.

Jax drew in a quick breath, reminding me that I was shamelessly running my hands over his naked torso. I cleared my throat and sat back. "That should do it."

"Almost." He took a small syringe from the pack and jabbed it into his own arm, barely blinking from the prick. "That should keep me from getting an infection from whatever I was exposed to on that Kronock ship." He shrugged back on his environmental suit but didn't wince as much as he had before.

A loud noise overhead made us both start. A ship was either hovering above us or was attempting to land.

"Is that—?" I asked, squinting out the front of the ship.

Jaxon hoisted the pack over one shoulder and grabbed my hand. "Our cue to run?" He opened the back hatch and pulled me through it with him. As soon as we stepped outside the ship, both of our boots sank into ground that felt more like a swamp. "It sure is."

CHAPTER
THIRTEEN

Jaxon

I pulled one boot from the murky mud and was met with a loud sucking noise. Peering through the crowded trees and dangling branches, I wondered if the entire moon was covered in this inky swamp. I didn't have too long to wonder before the roar of a ship's engine overhead made me crouch and Sam's hand twitch in mine.

For a moment, I'd forgotten that the woman was with me. The last thing I needed was to be dragging a human female around behind me, but I didn't have much choice. She *had* rescued me from the Kronock ship, and my Drexian honor wouldn't let me do anything less than protect her with my life. But why did she have to be human?

I glanced back at Sam as I tugged her behind me, my jerk on her hand rougher than I'd intended. Since the moon's surface was almost entirely black, not only was it hard to see her but our environmental suits adapted to the darkness, so that only her head was visible bobbing behind me.

With her choppy hair and heavily lined eyes, she looked nothing like any of the tribute brides I'd seen before, I'd give her that. My experience with the women from Earth had been limited to the few I'd seen during my one visit to the Boat. A visit I would rather not remember.

Letting out a dark grumble, I trudged forward, wading through the marsh instead of walking, and heading away from the Kronock ships circling above us. To her credit, Sam kept up with my fast pace, even though we were both breathing heavily after a while.

Once the engines were only a faint hum in the distance, I paused, dropping her hand and bracing my hands on my knees to catch my breath. The Drexian drugs might have helped but I still wasn't at my full strength.

"So, what's the plan?" She rested hands on her hips as she sucked in air. "We leg it away from the baddies and then what?"

Since our ship was all but destroyed, I didn't have much more of a plan than what she'd said, but she'd made it sound like not much of a strategy. I frowned as I looked up. "You have a plan you'd like to share?"

"This is my first space battle where I've ended up stuck on an enemy moon, so I haven't assessed the possibilities yet. I figure you've probably done stuff like this before."

I eyed her. "Get shot down and stranded on a Kronock moon? You think that's happened to me before?"

She twitched one shoulder. "You're Inferno Force, right? From what everyone says, you're the even tougher Drexians. Like Drexians, but on crack."

I tilted my head at her. "Crack?"

She flapped a hand at me. "Never mind." Then she stopped and narrowed her eyes at me. "Wait, are you telling me you've never done anything like this at all?"

"No." I wanted to laugh at the ridiculous look on her face. "Just because I'm Inferno Force doesn't mean I've been in enemy territory before. Being stranded on an alien moon isn't something that happens often—even if you're Inferno Force." I didn't add that I'd never seen a place like this, and that the eerie darkness of our surroundings was unsettling.

"Bollocks," she whispered. "So, this isn't something you trained for?"

Irritation flared in me. "I'm trained for plenty."

She shook her head. "Being one giant muscle doesn't mean much when it comes to survival. I've watched *Naked and Afraid*. How long can we even stay alive down here?"

One giant muscle? Naked and afraid? I cut my eyes to my nearly covered body. What was she talking about me? I patted the pack hooked over one shoulder. "I have rations and water for at least a few days."

Her gaze flitted to it, and she loosed a sigh "You do?"

"I wouldn't drag you off the ship and onto an alien environment without supplies." Especially an alien environment like this, I thought, suppressing a chill as a jet-black bug scampered down a tree truck covered in ebony, curling bark.

She unfastened the top of her environmental suit and rolled it down. "That makes me feel a bit better, but I still don't know where we're going."

"Away from the Kronock," I said. "We need to stay hidden until the Drexian fleet arrives."

"Does that mean we have to stay in these suits?" She

fanned her flushed face with one hand. "I don't know about you, mate, but I'm burning up."

She was right. The thick humid air had sweat rolling down my body—and I was only wearing the environmental suit. Sam had clothes on underneath hers.

"They do keep us masked." I glanced down at my suit, which had morphed to mirror the black jungle so that my body seemed to have vanished.

"But all the Kronock have to do is follow the floating heads." Sam pointed at her own head then at mine, which was the only part of me visible.

"We could put up our hoods."

She waved her hands in front of her. "No thank you."

I made my way to a fallen tree, sitting on the horizontal trunk so that it sank even farther and swinging my pack off my shoulder and onto the dark log beside me. As grateful as I was that the human had rescued me, I still couldn't wrap my head around the fact that Kalex had sent her in the first place. Since when did the Drexians use human females for military missions? Even the women who'd joined the crew of the Island weren't part of the military force. I cut my eyes to Sam, who was leaning up against a tree and swiping the back of her hand across her forehead. And this female wasn't even part of the military on Earth. What was this MI-6 she mentioned? It didn't sound comparable to Inferno Force.

How was I supposed to survive and keep her alive? Not only were humans smaller than Drexians, but they also weren't trained as warriors like we were. Especially not the females. The females were suitable as mates, but that was about it.

I opened my pack and found a water pouch. "You should drink."

Sam looked up, catching the pouch I tossed. She unscrewed the top and held the pouch high so that a stream poured into her mouth. Then she replaced the cap and tossed it back to me. "Thanks."

Before I could take a swig, a shadow descended quickly from above. I glanced up, expecting to see a Kronock ship. It wasn't a ship. It was a huge creature with papery wings the color of iron and the body of an insect. Red eyes flashed as it dove for me, its long beak open.

I flipped back off the log, hitting the ground as the creature's wings flapped and it landed on the fallen tree long enough to grasp my pack of supplies in its clawed feet and lift off again. Panic surged through me as I realized what was happening, and I jumped up.

I wasn't as fast as Sam, who'd leapt for the pack, clinging onto one of the straps as the creature flew higher. Instead of being pulled back down, the giant insect didn't seem to notice the extra weight, its wings beating the air as Sam's feet left the ground.

Grekking hell! I jumped up and wrapped my arms around Sam's waist. I could lose the pack. I couldn't lose another team member—even if it was a woman.

"Let go!" I yelled, yanking at her.

She looked down at me, her expression defiant at first. Then it softened, and she let go.

We both tumbled to the ground, hitting with a thud as mud splattered all over both of us.

I pushed myself up, wiping at the mud which only smeared it more. "What was that?"

She looked up at me, flecks of black all over her face. "I was trying to save our supplies."

"By getting dragged off by some alien beast?"

She frowned. "I thought he'd drop the pack."

I scraped a hand through my hair, no doubt streaking mud all through it. "You're lucky you aren't in some nest right now having your entrails picked out." I shook my head and peered up at the sky. "What did I do to deserve being saved by a human female?"

She stood up quickly. "What's that supposed to mean, 'a human female?' Do you have a problem with humans?"

I huffed out a hot breath. "I have no problem with humans."

"So, it's just women you don't like?" Her eyes were blazing now, and I suspected I'd made a big mistake.

"I don't *dislike* women. I just never thought I'd have to deal with one like this."

This was clearly a worse thing to say. She threw her hands up in the air. "Forgive me for risking my life to save your ass. I guess if I'd left you to rot in that cell you wouldn't have to deal with me."

"I didn't mean it like that," I growled.

She crossed her arms over her chest. "So, you meant 'deal with' in the extremely flattering way then? Like I need to deal with this herpes outbreak, or I need to deal with my two-year-old's temper tantrum?"

Now she was making no sense. I grabbed her by the sides of the arm. "I meant that I have to deal with the stress of being responsible for you."

"No one asked you to be responsible for me, you big

muppet. I'm a grown woman who's taken care of myself for most of my life. I don't need you."

My heart pounded as painful memories flooded my brain. Memories of another woman who'd told me she didn't want me. One who'd made it very clear she didn't need me by rejecting me entirely. I gritted my teeth. "Too bad. I'm Drexian, which means I'm going to protect you whether you want me to or not."

"I don't need anyone babysitting me, thank you very much." She spun around and started sloshing off through the swamp.

I let out an exasperated sigh, preparing myself to follow her, when she took a big step and sank beneath the surface of the black mud.

CHAPTER
FOURTEEN

Jaxon

y heart lurched as I watched the back of Sam's head drop and then vanish beneath the swampy surface. Without thinking, I dove forward, extending my arms down into the mud that gave way to liquid and finally dipping half my body into the muck.

I didn't dare open my eyes in the sludge, but instead, groped wildly. My fingers sifted through long grass and floating twigs before finally brushing across something feathery light. Hair! I stretched my arm farther and locked onto the collar of Sam's shirt. With a hard tug, I jerked myself from the water, pulling her with me.

Dragging her onto solid ground, I gasped for breath, as I flipped her limp body over on one side and pounded on her back.

Don't die on me. Please.

With a spasm, she spewed out a mouthful of brown water. After a long coughing fit, she finally cut her gaze to me. "It wasn't enough to drive me away. You had to beat me?"

"What?" I spluttered. "I wasn't beating—"

"Relax," she said, laughing through her coughs. "I was only taking the piss."

I shook my head, sinking back to the ground. I didn't understand what that meant or how she could be laughing. "You're okay?"

She crawled onto her hands and knees, her hair plastered to the side of her head, and heaved in some ragged breaths. "Only because you saved me. Thanks for that."

My face warmed even as I shrugged it off. "I owed you one."

Another laugh, this one not gurgling. "I guess you did." She peered at me and grinned. "But you look a lot worse after saving me than I did after saving you."

Now I laughed. "I didn't go falling into a swamp, did I? You only had to come onboard a Kronock battleship, which was devoid of mud."

"Fair enough." She sat back and swiped a dripping strand of hair off her forehead.

"Can we make a deal?" I asked, touching a hand to my aching ribs. Diving in after her hadn't helped with the residual pain, although the tape had held.

She eyed me. "The last deal I made is the reason I ended up having to break you from a Kronock ship."

"Can you try not to hitch a ride with alien monsters or fall into swamps for a while?"

She opened her mouth as if she was about to argue, then

clamped it shut and gave me a single nod. "If you promise not to make sexist comments about women."

I put a fist across my chest and thumped it to my heart. "Agreed."

She copied my movement. "Deal."

The sight of her attempting to return the Drexian salute in her soaking wet suit with her sopping hair and streaks of black running down her cheeks made the corners of my mouth twitch, so I quickly turned away before I laughed out loud.

I stood, letting the murky water sluice off my suit. Even though the fabric was constructed to be resilient, it wasn't waterproof without the hood being sealed, so I was soaked to the skin. Luckily, the moon was so steamy that I wasn't chilled, but it was still uncomfortable to be in a suit that was wet and hung heavy off my skin. I unfastened the top and tugged off the arms then started to roll it down my torso.

"What are you doing?"

I paused and looked up. "I'm taking this off. It's drenched."

She cut her eyes to the rainforest surrounding us. "You're going to walk around with nothing on?"

"I won't have nothing on." To be fair, my underwear was the dingiest thing I wore. If I should be getting rid of anything, it should be the black, ripped boxer briefs. Then I remembered something about humans. "Does me showing skin make you uncomfortable?"

She scoffed at this. "Don't be daft. You can show as much skin as you want. You have nothing I haven't seen before." Then her eyes widened. "Do you?"

I did grin at this, which made her scowl.

"You can walk around naked as far as I care, but I don't know if it's a good idea to be so exposed to the elements. And I thought you said the suit helps hide us?"

She made good points, but that didn't make me want to sit around in wet clothes. "As far as I can tell, the Kronock ships aren't searching near here anymore, so we're safe from them for now. I'll just take off the suit long enough for it to dry. Besides, this place is so dark, it's hard to imagine tracking down anything in it."

She glanced down at her own wet suit, the fabric now so heavy it looked like it was melting off her. "I wouldn't mind losing a layer."

Soon we were both peeling off the environmental suits and draping them over the fallen tree. It was so steamy that my damp skin didn't dry, though. The water droplets soon turned to beads of sweat that trailed down my muscles. I brushed them off, but more formed as quickly as I could flick them away.

When I looked up, Sam was staring at me, her mouth hanging open. "Sorry," she said when I caught her. "I didn't get a clear look at all your injuries in the darkness of the brig. How are you still walking around?"

I glanced at my bare flesh. She was right. The bruises that had seemed mild in the dim lighting on the Kronock ship looked violent and painful now. The dark forest might not have a lot of light, but it wasn't as shadowy as the Kronock cell, and the light that fought its way through the ebony tree branches seemed to illuminate my injuries. Even though she'd taped my torso, purple and blue swirled across my chest, punctuated with the occasional scorch mark from the electrodes, or an older bruise that was fading to a yellow hue.

There were lash marks across my legs and arms, as well as my back. Now that she'd reminded me, the dull ache of my ribs returned with a sharp ache. "I got used to the pain."

"You're sure that injection is all you need not to get an infection?"

I waved her concern away. "What we need to be thinking about is shelter."

"You mean like the ship?"

I narrowed my eyes at her. "I mean a place the enemy won't find right away."

One look at the sky told me that we wouldn't have much light left in the day. I didn't know what the Kronock moon was like at night—it was hard to imagine it getting any darker—but if the giant insect that had taken my pack was any indication, the place had more surprises waiting for us. And I did not want to be eaten in my sleep.

"What kind of shelter can we find on a place like this? It's all trees and water."

"We haven't seen all of it," I said, scooping up my suit and draping it over my shoulder. "I doubt that the entire moon is a swampland. We have to keep moving."

Sam jerked her thumb toward the spot where she fell into the water. "I don't recommend that way."

"Noted." I grabbed her suit and tossed it to her. "I suggest I take the lead."

She held up both hands. "You'll get no arguments from me."

I scooped up the water pouch, glad that at least we had that left, and started tramping forward. By my best guess, we didn't have long until night fell, and the moon became an entirely different—and more deadly—place.

CHAPTER
FIFTEEN

Samaira

"This isn't so bad." I eyed the makeshift awning constructed from broad, fan-shaped leaves that extended over the low hollowed-out rock. The dark leaves were layered on top of each other for added thickness and held up by a collection of branches burrowed into the ground, while inky vines were draped over the front to disguise it. I doubted it would hold up to much more than a strong gust of wind, but it was something.

After walking for what seemed like hours, the swamp had started to incline, and the ground had become more solid. When we'd stumbled onto a stream, we'd gratefully stopped to rest. It hadn't taken much more exploring to locate a rocky area near the stream—the stone a glossy obsidian that almost looked as if it had been polished—and then a small, hollowed out cave of sorts. It wasn't large enough to sit up in, but it was big enough for both of us to sleep under. When I'd pointed out how cozy we'd be, Jaxon had constructed the awning to extend the shelter.

I tried not to take it personally. The guy liked his own space. That wasn't unusual, although I'd have guessed that a military officer would have been used to close quarters.

He tilted his head up to the darkening sky. "It's almost night."

I sat down under the awning and crossed my legs. "Thank God. This has officially been the longest day ever."

Jaxon joined me on the ground, extending his long legs out in front of him and leaning back on his hands, the tattoos up one arm rippling as his forearms flexed. "You are thanking a deity for the natural cycle of a solar system?"

I'd tried not to stare at the bumps running down the length of his spine, which I knew were called nodes, but I was curious about them. Not curious enough to let on that I'd been looking at his mostly naked body. I'd gotten used to him wearing nothing but snug boxer briefs as he'd worked, but I did have to make a concerted effort to avert my eyes from the substantial bulge between his legs, especially now that he was sitting and leaning back. He seemed oblivious, though, and I remembered learning that Drexians had way fewer hang-ups about nudity than humans. That probably went double for Pakistani girls raised in London.

"It's just an expression," I said, looking into the sky as a glow of orange seeped up from the treetops and overtook the murky gray. "I don't know what I believe anymore when it comes to religion, but the more I see of the universe, the less I believe in the small gods we worship on Earth."

He nodded as if this made sense. "I must remember that

your planet is still primitive in many ways—along with your people."

What an ass. "You really are a sweet talker, Jaxon."

He lifted an eyebrow. "Everyone calls me Jax, and I don't think you meant that."

"Smart, too." I winked at him, pleased when his brow creased in obvious confusion.

We sat in silence for a few minutes as the day evaporated and an even more complete darkness enveloped the woods. The burbling of the stream was now joined by the chirping of insects and the distant cry of an alien animal. I shivered and rubbed my arms, amazed that Jax wasn't cold, considering he was in his skivvies.

My stomach growled, and I put a hand over it to mask the sound. There was no point in talking about how hungry we both were. The pack with rations was gone, and it wasn't safe to go back to the ship for more. Jax had made that perfectly clear when I'd brought up the subject earlier. Unfortunately, hunting and gathering wasn't part of my special skill set, and I wasn't sure if I felt confident eating food scavenged from an alien world. Not that we'd seen anything worth eating.

"You should get some sleep," he said. "I'll stay up and keep watch."

"Thanks, but I don't think I can sleep yet. It always takes me a while to unwind after a job, and this has been one hell of a job."

Jax grunted in acknowledgment of this. "I feel the same way after a battle. I need a shot of Noovian whiskey before I can release the stress and fall asleep."

"I've never tried Noovian whiskey, but right now, I'd drink anything if it would fill my stomach."

He snorted out a half laugh. "It would fill your stomach after burning it."

"Sounds perfect. My poison of choice was usually a nice gin and tonic, but a girl can't always be choosy. And I've pulled jobs in plenty of places where I drank whatever they had." I waved a hand at the black rainforest that was now draped in an additional layer of shadows. "None quite as rustic as this though or as black."

He nodded, the angles of his face even more striking in the darkness. "I've never been on a moon like this before. I wouldn't put it past the Kronock to have created this environment."

A shudder went through me. "For what purpose if no one lives here?"

Jax glanced at me, fear flickering in his eyes. "With the Kronock, you never know."

Well, that wasn't ominous.

Before I could tell him that his comments weren't making me feel any better, he cleared his throat. "Tell me about these jobs of yours. You work for your human government now, but you didn't always."

I circled my arms around my legs and rocked back, glad he couldn't see my face. "You're smarter than you look." This gained me a stifled guffaw. "And you're right. My holding a legitimate job is a new thing, and I've got to say, I'm not sure it's less dangerous than being a crook."

"When you say crook...?"

I drew in a breath, the air slightly cooler in the evening

but still humid and sticky. "I was a professional thief, a con artist, a cat burglar. Take your pick."

"You stole from people for a living?" He sounded startled by my admission, and I wondered how much crime there was in the Drexian world. I knew they'd done away with inequity in their society, which would have made crime less appealing. But still, there must be some like me who lived for the thrill of the con.

"Only bad people."

He leaned forward, his form an outline in the dark. "Explain."

"When I first started as a kid, I pulled whatever jobs my crew did. But when I got better and commanded my own crew, I decided that there were plenty of people who'd amassed wealth by taking advantage of those beneath them. It was easy to make a career of stealing from the rich robber barons of the modern age. What I took from them was still only a sliver of what they had, and they had what they had because they'd profited off others' toil and blood."

"What did you take?" He sounded interested now, and maybe a little impressed.

I clasped my hands together around my knees. "It might sound cliché, but my specialty was jewelry and art. If I happened upon piles of cash or gold bars, I didn't leave them behind, but I preferred to take the beautiful things they'd acquired to give a glittering sheen to their oppression and cruelty."

"Why?"

The single word question startled me. "What do you mean why? I told you why. They're bad people who did bad things to become rich."

"It wasn't personal?"

I flinched at this, his words like a barb reopening wounds that had long been healed—or so I thought. "My first job was my father's boss, the bloke who owned the factory where most men in our neighborhood worked. He was a horrible man who paid the least amount he could, cheated his workers on overtime, and forced them to work in a dangerous and outdated factory." My pulse fluttered as I thought back to sneaking into the man's opulent mansion. "I was young and untrained, so I hadn't learned how to open safes yet, but I did manage to sneak into his house and clear out his wife's jewelry and furs." I gave a dark laugh. "Turns out, most of the jewelry in her jewelry box was fake—costume stuff she wore for fun—but not all of it."

"And this was your job?"

"It was a good one, too."

"Not very honorable."

"You wouldn't say that if you knew more about the people I robbed. It's no different than you attacking the Kronock."

Even in the darkness, his stiffening shoulders were visible. "The Kronock are violent destroyers of civilizations."

"So were these people. They just did it more slowly and all while pretending to be respectable. The result is the same —ruined lives. I was righting wrongs, just like you."

He was silent for a beat. "You went about it in a strange way."

I shrugged. "I used my talents the best way I knew how. I didn't see you complaining about my criminal skills when I was breaking you from that cell."

A weary sigh. "I have a feeling I'm going to be hearing about that for a long time."

"Only until we get off this planet and back to Drexian space. Then you'll go back to being an Inferno Force pilot, and I'll go back to Earth, and you'll never have to be reminded of the time that a human female saved your ass."

"That cannot come fast enough."

I bristled at this. I'd just opened up to him, and this was what I got? "What gives?" I braced my hands on my thighs and leaned forward. "You clearly have a problem with me, and neither one of us is going to sleep until you tell me what it is."

"It's not you I have a problem with," he ground out the words. "It's *her*."

CHAPTER
SIXTEEN

Jaxon

"Her?" Sam asked, her sharp tone cutting through the night. "Who's her?"

I groaned. Talking about this was the last thing I wanted, but she had shared details of her past, so it was only fair I confessed why her presence bothered me so much. "The tribute bride I was matched with."

Silence stretched between us, the chirping and flowing water the only noises interrupting the heavy pause.

"You were matched with a tribute bride?" She sounded both shocked and disappointed. "So that's why you have such a problem with women? You didn't like the one they picked for you?"

Heat burned my cheeks, and I was grateful she couldn't see me. "It wasn't me who rejected her."

Another pause. "Tribute brides can reject Drexians? I didn't know that was a thing."

My heart thumped in my chest, the pain and rejection flaring as fresh inside me as they had the day I'd discovered the human I'd finally been matched with had decided not to take a mate. Although we'd never met, she had declined moving into a fantasy suite with me for our courtship and instead had chosen to live in a special section of the Boat with the other women who'd rejected their Drexians. "It is."

"I thought the whole deal with the tribute bride program was that women from Earth were taken and given to Drexians without their consent."

I scowled at this. "No female was ever forced. If she didn't want to be a tribute bride, she could opt to live in the reject section of the space station instead."

"The reject section?" Sam muttered. "Sounds like a party."

"They couldn't be returned to Earth since our existence wasn't common knowledge and we couldn't trust humans to be discreet, so they were given quarters together."

"But not one of those fancy holographic suites everyone talks about."

"No," I admitted, although I'd never spent a single night in the South Pacific wing of the station I'd planned to live on with my bride. "Not one of those. They were reserved for mated couples."

"Wait a second. If you were matched then that means at one point you wanted a human mate. You didn't always despise women."

I loosed a breath. "I told you before that I don't hate

women, but yes, I did sign up to be matched with a tribute bride. And waited for years."

"And then she didn't fancy you."

"Fancy?"

"Like. She didn't like you."

"I don't know if she would have liked me or not," I said. "We never met. I was on my way to the Boat to meet her when I received word that she'd decided not to accept the match. She didn't react well to learning about aliens and the space station and the tribute bride program. From what I understood, her background hadn't been fully researched. She didn't believe in scientific absolutes and refused to accept that aliens were real or that she was on a space station."

"Sounds like someone in recruiting made a total cock-up."

"It happened. Our research methods weren't foolproof, since we had to make sure not to alert humans to our presence. Our trips to Earth were infrequent and not all our agents were as diligent about their methods."

"That was when you snatched women from Earth and transported them in stasis, right?" Sam asked. "They'd wake up on the space station and learn that life as they'd always known it was over and they could never leave."

When she put it like that, it didn't sound so surprising that a woman might react badly.

Sam let out a low whistle. "I'm surprised you got as many takers as you did."

"It's an honor to be a tribute bride for a Drexian warrior," I said, squaring my shoulders and repeating the mantra I'd heard most of my life. "The women we took from Earth never had families or many friends. The lives they had on the Boat were much better."

"Even so, not everyone likes to be saved." She cleared her throat pointedly.

I ignored this comment. "The brides who rejected their mates have all been given the option to return to Earth since the Big Reveal. Only a few have chosen to leave."

"What about your bride? Did she go back?"

"She was never my bride," I snapped, then regretted my harsh tone and softened it. "I don't know what she did. I didn't ask."

"Why didn't you get the next bride? It wasn't like they matched you based on personality, right? It was more the luck of the draw since you were pulling from such a limited pool of women."

I shook my head. "I didn't want another match. I was soured on the idea of a human female if one had rejected me without even meeting me. It struck me that humans must be difficult and close-minded, so I chose to throw myself into my career in Inferno Force. I haven't regretted my decision."

"Except you're clearly still upset about it if you can't even stand the sight of a human female."

I bit back a sharp response. Maybe she was right. When I'd seen Sam standing outside my cell and realized she was human, I'd had a visceral reaction. And not a good one.

"I might have been carrying old grievances that had nothing to do with you."

"You think?" she said under her breath, but loud enough for me to hear.

My mouth twitched into a grin despite my instinct to be annoyed with her. No one could claim that this woman was close-minded, especially since she herself operated on the outside of human norms. And she wasn't fearful of the unknown, since she'd snuck onto a Kronock battleship with almost no military training. But I wasn't ready to concede that she wasn't difficult. Not that I didn't begrudgingly admire that about her, too.

Sam let out a long breath. "We both had preconceived ideas coming into this. I assumed all Drexians were cocky and obnoxious. You thought all human women were high-maintenance and unwilling to open their minds to new ideas and possibilities. Clearly, you were wrong."

"Just me?" I asked, hearing the teasing tone in her voice.

"Fine, you're not quite as obnoxious as you were when we met. But you're still a cocky sod."

"I'm not cocky. I'm confident."

"Same difference. If you were in nursery, they'd say you don't play well with others."

"Says the woman who prefers to work alone."

"If I work alone, I'm the only one who can get hurt." Her voice cracked. "My job is dangerous, and I can't live with risking any life but my own."

As a member of Inferno Force who risked his life on every mission, I understood this fear perfectly. I also knew it was an impossibility if I wanted to be a part of a team. "You lost someone?"

"A long time ago when I was too young and foolish to understand the risks. So was he, but he got himself killed, and I got away."

"So, you isolated yourself to make sure that never happened again?"

"It worked. I've never lost anyone since."

"Because you have no one to lose." I couldn't imagine life without my Inferno Force brothers. We lived as one unit—fighting and dying together. "You've been alone."

"I've had a mission, Jax. Sometimes those have to be carried out alone."

"There's no room for vigilantes in the Drexian empire, Sam."

She let out a rueful laugh. "Then there's no room for me."

There was a strange pang in my gut as I thought about her leaving Drexian space once her mission was over. It was true that I hadn't welcomed her help or her rescue, but I also hadn't met a female so interesting in quite a while. As fun as the pleasurers on the pleasure planets were, I rarely talked to them beyond commands or requests, and their responses were rarely more than a few breathy words, usually asking for it harder or faster.

Sam was different. She was irritating, but she was also complicated and intriguing. I'd never met an actual thief before, and I was surprised to find that I could relate to her more than I would have thought possible.

"Don't move," she whispered, rocking forward slowly.

Before I could compute what she was doing, her hand had darted out and slapped at something over my shoulder. The momentum from her fast movement propelled her onto me, and with a yelp, she fell forward and into my lap. She attempted to scramble back but her awkward movements only resulted in her groping me almost everywhere.

"What the *grek*?" I grasped her by the waist if only to keep her from flailing against me and hitting my bruises.

"There was a huge insect slithering toward you from one of the hanging vines. I saw the shadow on your shoulder," she said, panting when she finally stopped floundering. She was still practically on top of me, her knees straddling my waist and her face within inches of mine.

I twisted my head, shivering instinctively at the thought.

"It's gone. I swatted it away, and I'm sure all our moving scared it off." She'd stilled in my grip, and her breathing was shallow. "Do you want to let me go?"

I dropped my gaze to where my hands spanned her waist. I was holding her on top of my cock, which had stiffened and was about to burst from my frayed underwear. I didn't want to let her go. As maddening as the female was, she also stirred something deep inside me that hadn't truly awakened in a long time. My gaze locked on her eyes glittering in the darkness then drifted to the curve of her lips. Even though we were both sweaty and had been drenched in swamp water, I was overcome with the pounding desire to taste her.

"Jax?" She wiggled on my lap, which did nothing to help my aching cock.

I tore my gaze from her alluring lips and loosened my grip on her. "Sorry. Thanks for keeping the creature from landing on me."

She scrambled off me, not meeting my eyes. "Don't mention it. I'll add it to your tab." She yawned pointedly. "I'm done in. You sure you're okay taking the first watch?"

"I'm sure," I said, grateful when she crawled into the low, open cave and stretched out. I shifted myself so that I was sitting directly in front of the rock opening, leaning my head against the hard, smooth overhang.

Soon her breathing was deep and even, as she slipped into sleep. My breathing was not, my pulse racing from being so close to the woman, and the disturbing realization that I wanted nothing more than to curl up next to her and claim her as mine.

Grek.

CHAPTER
SEVENTEEN

Samaira

I flattened my back against the wall, my eyes adjusted to the darkness as we moved on silent feet through the ornate house. Some burglars used night vision goggles, but I didn't believe in the things. They were brilliant for detecting movement, but not good for assessing the quality of jewels. That, and they were one more thing to carry on a job. I preferred to travel light.

The finger brushing mine made me jump, and I swiveled my head. Rayan stood only an inch or so shorter than me, but with his dark hair and eyes—and both our heads covered by black caps—we could have passed as twins. It didn't matter that he was a fifteen-year-old boy, and I was nearly twenty.

I put a finger to my lips, and he nodded, his eyes glittering with excitement. It was our first job together, and our first job independent of our usual team. Even though we'd grown up in the same East London neighborhood and even lived in the same council terrace houses, we hadn't become friends until we'd started pulling jobs together. I was the veteran, skilled at sneaking past security systems and opening safes, and he was the apprentice, eager to learn so he could move past the usual snatch-and-grabs that were the staple of most thieves.

But I wasn't most thieves. I had no interest in robbing middle-class homes and carting off electronics that were more trouble to fence than they were worth. I targeted the wealthy—the houses with high-tech security and safes hidden behind overpriced art—and only took the ostentatious adornments of their status.

Slipping through the foyer and around a marble table that held an urn bursting with fragrant lilies, I led us into the study. I'd done my homework and my reconnaissance. This was where the bank CEO kept what was important to him.

I motioned to Rayan to follow me as I padded across the plush Persian carpet covering the office floor. I wasn't worried about anyone upstairs waking up and surprising us. The bank CEO and his wife were on holiday in the Seychelles. The only person at home was the housekeeper, and she'd snuck out earlier to see her boyfriend. What made this even easier was the fact that the owners weren't pet people, so there were no dogs to be alerted to our presence. I hated having to sedate animals and usually avoided homes with dogs.

Should have learned to live with the dog hair, I thought about the unguarded house as I ran my gloved finger along the leather spines of the books in the floor to ceiling bookcase. When I reached the right book, I pulled it forward, holding my breath for a beat as the bookcase slid back to reveal a gunmetal-gray safe large enough to hold a person. Or a lot of valuables.

Beside me, Rayan inhaled quickly. I stole a quick glance at him, winking.

Even through the snug leather, my fingers tingled as I touched the lock. Without wasting any time, I pulled my stethoscope up and put the earpieces in before pressing the bell end to the steel surface of the safe. I rested my forehead against the cold metal beside the stethoscope as I began to turn the lock, holding my breath and listening for the clicks and pops but also feeling the vibrations through my head.

Like I'd taught him, Rayan was silent beside me. His job was to listen for any movement within the house or outside while I concentrated fully on the safe. Despite disabling the alarm system, I never discounted the possibility of being surprised. No matter how much I planned, life always threw curves. The difference between the great burglars and the ones sitting in jail was the ability to anticipate the curves.

A few deft turns later, I was releasing my breath, wiping off any trace of my forehead touching the safe, and pulling open the heavy door. Even in the shadowy room, I sucked in a sharp breath when I saw the stacks of currency piled high. For a bank CEO, this guy didn't seem to believe in keeping his money in them.

I turned to nudge Rayan, but he was already holding the black backpack open, his eyes wide. I quickly emptied the safe of its cash, adding a couple of expensive watches to our haul. I ignored the handguns—firearms weren't something I dealt in or wanted to touch—signaling to Rayan to zip up the pack.

Then my eyes lit on a manila envelope on the shelf at the top. Documents in safes were usually very boring—wills, titles to cars and houses—or very incriminating. Knowing what I did about the CEO who'd risen to power by taking over smaller banks and firing all their employees, I hoped it was the latter. I shoved it into the inside of my jacket, closing the safe as silently as I'd opened it.

Rayan swung the backpack onto his shoulder, grinning at me. I returned his grin, no doubt feeling the same thrill he was at how smoothly the job had gone and how much we'd gotten. I led the way from the office and back through the foyer, breathing in the scent of lilies that I'd always loved. That was when the pop made me jump.

Spinning around, I saw a man standing in the doorway underneath the sweeping staircase. He was in a checked shirt and had dark, shaggy hair. The housekeeper's boyfriend, I thought, my research rushing back to me. He wasn't supposed to be here. Neither was his gun.

I cut my eyes to Rayan. "Run!"

We both took off across the marble floor as a second shot rang out. Tearing through the dining room and kitchen, I could hear heavy, booted footfalls behind us as the man gave chase. I burst from the French doors, not bothering to be quiet anymore. Rayan was right on my heels when he slipped and hit the hard tile of the kitchen floor. The backpack slipped off his shoulder and skidded a few feet away.

I jerked him to his feet. "Forget it."

He hesitated, pulling away from me and reaching for the bag. Then the gunshot tore through his neck, spinning him in place and sending blood spattering across my face. When he hit the floor, his eyes were already wide and unseeing. For a beat, the world froze, and all I could see were his blank eyes and the blood puddling around his dark hair. Another shot snapped me from my trance as it whizzed by my ear. Staggering back, I stumbled from the house and ran across the alabaster patio, glancing back once to see my bloody footprints making a black trail across the marble.

My heart hammered wildly as I choked back sobs and ran as fast as I could, jumping over hedges and clambering over fences until I was far enough away that I was sure I hadn't been followed. When I finally made my way home through every back alley and darkened street in the city, I sobbed until my throat was raw.

It was all my fault that Rayan was dead. He was just a kid and now he was lying dead in some rich wanker's kitchen. How had I made such a fatal error?

"Never again," I chanted over and over to myself. I would never lose anyone again.

"Sam." My memories evaporated as I was jerked from sleep, although the hot tears sliding salty between my lips were as real as they always were. I didn't have time to get my bearings or figure out who was whispering my name before a strong hand was clamped over my mouth and a thick arm snaked around my waist.

CHAPTER
EIGHTEEN

Jaxon

The sounds of the alien rainforest were so rhythmic and soothing that it was hard not to nod off as I sat in front of the low, open mouthed cave. The only thing keeping me awake and alert was the presence of Sam sleeping soundly behind me. Even though I faced forward, I could hear her soft breathing, and I imagined I felt the heat of her body. Knowing that I was within an arm's reach of the human was enough to jangle my nerves and keep me alert.

I let out a huff of breath. Why was my body suddenly reacting to her? I'd never felt this rattling of nerves with a female before, not even with the most striking of alien pleasurers. I'd also never gotten to know any of the females I'd hired to pleasure me, beyond what made them moan and come.

Sam intrigued me. She was more complex than I'd imagined a human could be, which made me want to know more about her. And her desire to work alone and keep everyone at a distance made her a greater challenge. I'd always relished a challenge.

I shook my head. Was I *grekking* insane? Sam had been sent on a mission to rescue me. Once the mission was over, she'd be gone. She was also a human female, and I'd sworn off human females for good. There was nothing about this that was a good idea. So why could I think about nothing but the pretty human with the light-brown skin and thickly lashed dark eyes?

At least she looked nothing like the image of the human woman I'd been matched with. My stomach lurched even now as I remembered how many times I'd stared at the image of the female with pale hair and a smattering of dots they called freckles across her nose, convinced she was my true mate. I didn't know if they'd shown her my image, but I didn't want to know. It had been hard enough to be rejected. I couldn't take the thought that she'd seen me as well. It was better to think I'd been rebuffed sight unseen.

But Sam was nothing like the other woman—not in appearance and not in any other way. The human who'd rejected being matched with me had been terrified of the unknown, while Sam had willingly flown into alien space to save me. True, she hadn't been given much of a choice, but she'd had a choice, and she'd chosen the unknown.

"She's nothing like her," I insisted, as if my fervent whispers would make it true. "Nothing."

I was so caught up in my thoughts that I almost didn't hear it the first time. But the second branch that snapped had me on high alert.

Someone was walking through the forest. More cracks shot through the quiet as the sound got closer. Multiple someones—and they weren't small creatures. Their footfall wasn't tentative as they tramped through the underbrush.

My heart lurched in my throat as I attempted to peer through the darkness, the light of another, far off moon providing the only illumination. If only everything wasn't as inky as the night, I thought, my eyes aching as I tried to squint hard enough to differentiate between the shades of black. Even so, I couldn't make out anything but vague shapes. But the shapes weren't comforting, nor were the occasional flashes of gray. I was confident it was the Kronock.

Since I didn't know how many enemy soldiers were in pursuit, and I didn't like my odds of a firefight in the dark, I flattened myself against the rock and slid under the over-hang. It was large enough to cover two bodies, but barely. I moved as far underneath as I could, my body pressing up against Sam's warm one.

Before Sam could wake up and make a sound, I clapped a hand over her mouth, wrapping another around her body to keep her from flailing or making a noise that might alert the enemy to our presence.

"Sam," I whispered. She jerked awake, but I put my mouth to her ear. "Don't move. We're being hunted."

Even though her body had tensed, she stilled, going silent and finally nodding. I kept my hand over her mouth, if only because any movement created sound, and the Kronock footsteps—and the noise of their heavy tails dragging behind them—were almost on top of us.

"This is the second one in this solar cycle," a rough voice

said, cutting through the quiet of the night.

There was a grunt of reply followed by the caw of a distance bird. "Not our fault."

I held my breath as the voices stopped so close to where we were hiding I suspected they were near enough to touch. When the makeshift awning collapsed, I braced myself to be dragged from beneath the rock, but they didn't seem to notice. In the dark—and because everything was as black as the night—the leaves and branches must have appeared as more underbrush.

One of the Kronock snorted in a breath. "They won't be happy."

"We'll find him one way or the other. There's nowhere for him to run."

My stomach clenched, and Sam's body stiffened against mine. The thought of being trapped on the Kronock moon with nowhere to run wasn't a pleasant one. At least they were only looking for me. They didn't seem to know about Sam, which gave us an advantage, even if it was slight.

"I'm not staying out here all night searching again," one of the Kronock said with a grunt.

"You want to tell them he got away?"

Feet stamped roughly in the leaves, kicking a few into the cave.

"He can't get away. If he's stuck out here, he's as good as dead. The little alien scum won't be able to survive for more than a few rotations."

My heart pounded, and I could swear I felt Sam's thudding heartbeat as well. I tightened my grip on her, her body comforting even as I was aware that I'd crossed a line by embracing her. My large hand was pressed against her stomach, the tips of my fingers brushing the swell of her breasts, but I didn't move it. Holding her was helping me hold my sanity together, as the terrifying thought of being tortured by the enemy filled my mind with the sounds of my own screams. I couldn't force myself to loosen my grip or roll away from her. Not when the enemy was right on top of us, and I was fighting against panic that clawed wildly at my throat.

If only she didn't feel so good in my arms, the skin at the nape of her neck soft and her ass pressed up against my cock. I closed my eyes and tried to concentrate on calming my jangling nerves, but my body hummed with unwanted desire, every part of me hardening with need that had quickly overtaken my panic and fear as my lips feathered the back of her neck.

Sam must have felt the shift in me, because she elbowed me in the ribs.

A Kronock gave a sharp, mirthless laugh, which masked my stifled groan. "Then we can come back during the day and collect the corpse."

"I like that plan."

I dared to twist my head around and peer from the low opening. I couldn't see much, but I did see clawed, scaly feet and long batons of some kind swinging beside them. The ends of the batons were rounded with sharp spikes that glinted in the dim moonlight. I'd never seen the Kronock brandish these weapons, although nothing about the enemy could surprise me anymore.

The two Kronock moved away, crashing through the underbrush as they went. I allowed myself to release a breath, and Sam did the same. After a little while longer, and once the guttural Kronock voices had faded, she shifted in my arms.

"I think you can let go of me now."

I immediately uncoiled my arm from her and scooted from the cramped cave. I stood and scanned the dark forest, but there was no movement or noises aside from the insects and animals that lived there. The cacophony of chirping and hooting was a welcome return after the harsh voices of the Kronock.

"They're gone," I said over my shoulder.

Sam crawled from the cave and joined me. "What the bloody hell was that?"

"At least two Kronock," I said, "but they were carrying weapons I haven't seen them use before. Maybe they're a special patrol unit."

"Not that, Jax." She crossed her arms, her annoyance evident even in the dark. "I mean, you grabbing me. You're lucky those two creeps were so close, or I would have done more than elbow you."

An unpleasant heat prickled up my neck. "I apologize. I initially wanted to alert you to the Kronock presence without you making any sudden noises."

"Mmhmm. I've heard that before."

"You've had someone quiet you so you wouldn't alert enemy aliens before?"

"Not that exactly, but I know when I'm being fed an excuse."

Now I folded my arms across my chest. "You believe I conjured the Kronock to have an excuse to keep you quiet?"

"Maybe you didn't conjure them, but you used their appearance to your advantage."

I bristled at this, even as I wondered if she was right. Then I shook my head. No, I never would have touched her if the aliens hadn't appeared. And if there had been any other way to wake her without fear of her making noise, I would have done that. Irritation flared inside me, and I remembered why I'd wanted to steer clear of the female. "I do not need to contrive an excuse to touch a female. I have plenty of females very willing for my touch."

"I'll bet you do. I've heard plenty about how the Drexians entertain themselves before they take mates."

I almost moaned out loud, this time from exasperation. "In case you weren't listening, the enemy is searching for me. If they catch me, they catch you, and that will be bad for both of us. I'm sorry if you were offended by my method of keeping you quiet, but I hope you understand that me holding you for a few moments isn't a fraction as torturous as what you'll experience if the Kronock take you prisoner."

She was quiet for a beat, possibly contemplating Kronock torture. "I don't think they were looking for you."

Even though she couldn't see my face well in the dark, I gaped at her. "What do you mean? Of course, they were looking for me."

"Didn't you hear what they said? They called you a little alien. Now don't let it go to your head, but no one would call a Drexian little. Even the Kronock."

I hadn't focused on that detail, but now that she mentioned it, the phrasing did seem odd. "If they're not looking for an escaped Drexian who crashed on their moon, who the *grek* are they looking for?"

"I think that would be me," a tiny voice piped up from above.

CHAPTER
NINETEEN

Samaira

J ax and I both jumped, looking up into the dark treetops soaring above us. It was nighttime, but faint moonlight filtered through the canopy of leaves and made it possible for me to detect some shapes.

"Who's there?" Jax asked, his tone commanding as he assumed a fighting position with his arms up.

"Oh, dear," said the voice. "I assure you I'm not a threat."

I honed in on the squeaky voice, my gaze settling on a small figure perched on a tree limb overhead. He wasn't large, and he wasn't Kronock. "Who are you?"

"I'd be happy to come down and introduce myself if you can assure me that your big friend is tame."

I snorted out a laugh as Jax relaxed his pose. "I don't know about tame, and at the moment I'm not sure if we're friends either. He is Drexian, so that means he's a cocky git, but I promise he won't hurt you."

Jax grunted at this but didn't correct me.

"Very well," the creature said, as he climbed down from the tree, landing between us and straightening to his full height, which still only brought him to Jax's waist.

From his shadow and the glimmers of light creeping through the leaves, I could make out short hair that looked purple and a humanoid body about two-thirds my size. His arms and legs were proportional, and unlike some of the aliens I'd seen on the Drexian space station, he had no tail or horns.

"You're Gatazoid," Jax said, the surprise evident in his tone.

The little alien bowed. "Fillian, at your service."

"I'm Jaxon, but my friends call me Jax." The Drexian thumped a fist to his chest.

"Are we friends?" Fillian asked in a hushed voice.

"Well, we're both clearly on the run from the Kronock. I think that makes us friends."

"My first Drexian friend," Fillian said, then turned to me. "And what are you?"

"Human," I said, once I realized that he wasn't asking my profession. "My name is Samaira, but anyone who wants to live calls me Sam."

Fillian emitted a tiny squeak. "Then I will most certainly call you Sam, Miss Samaira."

Jax hid a laugh behind his hand, which I chose to ignore.

"Gatazoid? Is that a species of alien?" I was still adjusting to the concept of aliens existing altogether. Sometimes I was startled to realize how many other species existed outside of Earth, and how clueless my planet had been.

"Gatazoids were decimated by the Kronock a while ago," Jax said. "Now those who remain work with us on space stations, colonies, or outposts."

"I think I met one when I arrived on the space station. He claimed to be a wedding planner and tried to talk me into being a tribute bride."

"That sounds like Serge," Jax said.

"The Drexians saved us," Fillian said. "If it wasn't for them, we would be nomads wandering through space."

"Humans aren't the first species we've fought the Kronock to protect," Jax added. "We haven't always been successful, but we've always provided refuge for aliens who are victims of our enemy. Just like the Boat, the Island will be staffed with aliens from across the galaxy who no longer have a home."

I had to admit that was pretty cool. If I was a badass alien species, I'd want to offer a better life to alien refugees, too. I shifted from one foot to the other. Maybe the Drexians weren't just arrogant warriors with a hard-on for battle and anything female.

"We're a people known for our talents as artisans." Fillian's small chest puffed out as he spoke. "We work as chefs, or artists, or designers."

"You haven't lived until you've eaten a meal cooked by a Gatazoid chef," Jax said.

Fillian giggled. "You're too kind."

"So how did a Gatazoid end up on a Kronock moon deep in Kronock space?" I asked.

"Like I mentioned before, Gatazoids are artisans. I was

trained to be a chef of sweets, which isn't always in high demand in the Drexian world."

"A pastry chef?" I asked, my stomach growling at the mere thought of food. "How could a pastry chef not be in high demand? Everyone loves dessert, right?"

"Sugar isn't widely used in Drexian cuisine," Jax said, "although our connection with humans has made it more of a presence."

"Especially when human females are expecting a child." Fillian giggled once more. "Then sweets chefs are highly valued."

"I'll bet," I said. Personally, I couldn't imagine a life without sugar, especially chocolate.

"I was en route to a new posting at a Drexian colony," Fillian continued. "One with lots of human-Drexian couples, so plenty to keep me busy. But our transport was attacked by the Kronock."

"I heard about that attack," Jax muttered. "I thought everyone on board was killed."

Fillian sighed, pulling a square of fabric from his clothing and dabbing his eyes. "The Drexians were, but the Kronock commander who led the boarding party recognized me as a Gatzoid." He swallowed hard. "He knew of our talents and demanded that I come serve under him."

"The Kronock eat dessert?" I asked. The idea that the huge, scaled beasts would have the need for a chef—much less a pastry chef—seemed incongruous to me.

"I don't think he cared that my specialty is sweets." Fillian's tone darkened. "All he cared about was me serving under him as his personal slave."

"That's awful," I said, reaching out and touching the alien's arm.

"Considering the Kronock, I'd say he was going easy on you," Jax said.

"Perhaps, but I refused." The Gatazoid jammed the cloth back in his pocket. "I might not be a fierce warrior, but I have my pride, and I won't be anyone's slave. I'd rather die."

Fillian's courage surprised me, although it shouldn't have. I'd learned long ago that size and physical strength didn't imbue a person with courage. Some of the bravest people I'd known had been the least assuming.

"But they didn't kill you," Jax said.

Fillian shook his head. "Some days I wish they had. Death would have been quicker."

"The Kronock do enjoy their torture," Jax said so quietly his words disappeared on a gust of wind.

"I take it you've experienced Kronock punishment?" Fillian asked.

Jaxon didn't reply right away.

"He was being held prisoner on a Kronock battleship," I said, so he wouldn't need to explain. "I was part of the Drexian rescue team sent in to break him out. The two of us are all that's left of the team."

"You broke him from a Kronock brig? I didn't know human females were such great warriors. I have only heard of them being excellent tribute brides."

I fought the urge to snap back a snarky reply, but it wasn't Fillian's fault that all he knew about women was our ability as mates for Drexians. "I'm not a warrior, but I'm definitely not a tribute bride."

"Fascinating." Fillian tapped one short finger against his

chin. "You might not be a warrior, but if you can break a Drexian from a Kronock brig, you must be extremely clever."

"She's a thief," Jax said.

Fillian inhaled sharply, as if I'd just been revealed as a deranged criminal.

"He's right," I said, squaring my shoulders. "I'm what we call a cat burglar. I specialize in sneaking into heavily guarded places and taking valuables from wealthy villains."

"You steal from villains?" Fillian's tone was curious. "That doesn't sound so bad."

I shot Jax a murderous glare, even though he couldn't see it. "I like to think of it as righting wrongs and restoring balance in the world, kind of like what the Drexians do when they fight the Kronock. Or like what I did when I snuck onto an enemy ship and took their prisoner out from under their nose."

"Then you might be just the two to help me."

My eyes had adjusted enough to the darkness that I could see that Fillian wore a utilitarian jumpsuit that was torn and dirty and no shoes on his stubby feet.

"You're more than welcome to come with us when we're rescued," Jax said, although you still haven't told us how you ended up on an uninhabited Kronock moon."

"Rescued?" Fillian clapped his hands together. "Do you really think you'll be rescued?"

"The Drexians will come for us," Jax said, not a shred of doubt in his voice.

"That's the best news I've heard since I was taken by the Kronock and brought here." Fillian sighed and ran a hand through his choppy hair.

I glanced around the dense forest. "And how long have

you been here? A deserted moon seems a strange place to bring a prisoner."

"This isn't just a Kronock moon, and it's far from deserted." Fillian said, shaking his head. "This is a black moon."

Jax and I both stared at him, waiting for him to elaborate.

"Sorry," I finally said. "I'm human, remember? What does that mean, a black moon?"

"A black Kronock moon—a prison moon."

CHAPTER
TWENTY

Jaxon

My skin went cold as I processed the Gatazoid's words. "Prison moon?"

Fillian's large round eyes were luminous, as he shifted his gaze from me to Jax and back to me. "You truly didn't know?"

Icy tendrils of fear slid across my skin, making me shiver despite the warm, humid air. "We were unaware that the Kronock kept entire moons for the sole purpose of housing prisoners." Although, as soon as I said it, it sounded just like what our enemy would do.

"Why are they black?" Sam asked. "Aside from it being bloody creepy?"

"Almost everything on the surface on a black moon is dead or deadly," Fillian said. "You can't eat any of the plants, and the few animals that can survive here are vicious—or venomous. If one of the prisoners escapes, we usually don't last long."

"What about the water?" I asked, thinking of the amount Sam and I had both swallowed when she'd taken a fall into the swamp.

"I suspect that's fine, otherwise it would kill all the creatures," Fillian shuddered and glanced around him, "and they seem to be abundant."

I was only a bit relieved. Fillian was right. The moon was crawling with creatures, and knowing they were deadly didn't help.

"Well, that's just brilliant," Sam muttered. "We crashed on the only moon that could actually kill us."

"This isn't the only one," Fillian said. "At least according to the guards. I've heard them talk about transferring to a black moon prison that isn't subterranean."

"Subterranean?" Sam's voice cracked. "The prison is underground?"

The Gatazoid bobbed his head up and down. "That's why I'd rather be up here on the surface, even though it is hot and swampy, with killer bugs the size of Zerillian hawks. It's a relief to see the sky."

I gulped. If the Gatazoid preferred being on the surface —*this* surface—to being in the prison, what must it be like underground? I hadn't spent long in the Kronock cell, but even that had felt like an eternity to be in the dark with no windows and no way to know how much time was passing. I tried to imagine being trapped in an underground prison— essentially buried alive—and the thought made my throat constrict.

"How big is the prison?" I forced myself to speak.

Fillian rubbed his arms briskly, and I wondered if the memories of the prison he'd escaped from were making him cold. "I'm sure I didn't see all of it, but it's no small thing. There must be hundreds of prisoners spread out throughout the underground maze."

"Hundreds?" Sam's voice echoed the horror that I felt.

"Who are these prisoners?" I asked. What I really wanted to know was why the Drexian High Command hadn't heard of these prison moons before. The Kronock had always been secretive, and they'd gone dormant for years, and then quiet again after their failed attack on Earth. Regardless, prison moons housing hundreds of captives was something we should have known about—especially if citizens under our protection were being held in them.

"Mostly aliens from planets resisting their invasions," Fillian said.

"But if the Kronock find resistance, they usually stamp it out by killing the offenders," I argued. "They've never been known for taking prisoners en masse like this."

Unless they were changing their tactics, I thought with a sinking feeling in my gut. One thing we'd learned since our enemy had reappeared after years of perceived slumber, the Kronock were constantly adapting to become more brutal oppressors and invaders. They must believe that keeping prisoners was advantageous to them, or they wouldn't bother doing it. The Kronock had no problem committing murder, so they must view the prisons as a tactical maneuver.

"So, these are political prisoners?" I asked. "Not criminals?"

Fillian twitched his small shoulders. "I wasn't aware of

any criminals. Mostly aliens who'd said the wrong thing or dared to defy the Kronock."

"Tell me more about this prison." I sat down and patted the floor next to me to indicate that the Gatazoid should join me. "You said it's underground."

He sat, folding his legs in front of him. "I think the surface of the moon is too marshy and unstable for them to build on, so they dug down."

Not to mention, the swampy surface made it harder when prisoners did escape. It wasn't easy to run through a virtual bog, especially one designed to poison you. I wondered if the water was deadly, and my throat tightened.

"Where is the entrance?"

Fillian swiveled his head around as if he was looking for it. "It's hard to say for sure since I wasn't paying attention to direction when I ran, but it's over there somewhere." He swung a leveled finger in the opposite direction of where our ship had crashed.

I nodded. "That makes sense. That's the direction the two Kronock walked in after they stopped here."

"They're two of the lazier ones," Fillian said. "I was lucky the others weren't sent out after me."

I tried not to think about the Kronock guards. Instead of the few I'd assumed had been sent down to the moon's surface to look for me, I now knew that there were many more guarding a secret prison.

"What type of entrance does it have? Is it well hidden or easy to find?"

Sam tapped one of her feet on the ground. "Why are you asking so much about the prison?"

I peered up at her. The woman's profile was in shadow,

but it was clear she was narrowing her eyes at me. "Aren't you curious?"

"These aren't questions you ask because you're curious," she said, her foot tapping faster. "They're questions you ask when you're casing a joint."

"Casing a joint?" Yet another human phrase that confused me.

"Learning about a building so you can assess its weaknesses," she said. "You know, before you break into it."

"You think I—"

"Oh, I know you do, Jax," she cut me off. "I can hear it in your voice. You can't stand the thought of innocent creatures being held against their will, so you think you should get them out."

I stood quickly. "What if I do?"

"Just because you're a Drexian, and you're known for protecting the galaxy from the Kronock, doesn't mean you have to singlehandedly break into an underground prison."

"Why doesn't it?" My voice was vibrating with frustration. "If I can't help others who are in need or who are being abused, then what point is there to be a Drexian warrior? I didn't join Inferno Force to run away from things that were hard, or only go on missions that were easy." I took a breath. "And who said I'd be doing it alone?"

Her eyebrows shot up and she began to shake her head so hard her damp hair slapped the sides of her cheeks. "No bloody way. I literally just broke you from one Kronock jail, and now you want to crawl back in another?"

"I don't *want* to."

She held my gaze until she finally let out a whoosh of breath, and her shoulders drooped. "You have to, right?

You'll never live with yourself if you don't try to save these prisoners?"

"Kind of like you have to steal things from people who deserve to be punished," I said.

She pursed her lips. "Low blow, mate."

I shrugged, not sorry that I'd made her see that we weren't so different after all, and not sorry that I'd realized it.

"I beg your pardon," Fillian said. "Are you two talking about going into the prison?"

"We can't leave those prisoners to the mercy of the Kronock," I said, as the alien wrung his hands together.

"I just got out." His voice trembled. "I can't go back."

Sam rested a hand on his shoulder. "We would never ask you to do that. Besides, you're not a professional lunatic like Jax here."

"Says the woman who crawled through a Kronock venting system to find me."

"What can I say? I love vents."

Fillian looked back and forth between us, his eyes unblinking. "I'm starting to think finding you two wasn't the advantage I first thought it was."

Sam barked out a laugh, but then lowered herself to the ground beside Fillian and patted his leg. "I have no intention of making you go anywhere near that prison again, and we promise that when we get off the moon, we're taking you with us."

This seemed to mollify him. "Thank you. I can't tell you how relieved I am to hear that, but do you still intend to sneak into the prison?"

Sam gave me a stern look. "I think we can all agree that it would be foolish to attempt to rescue potentially hundreds of prisoners by ourselves." When I opened my mouth to speak, she held up a palm to silence me. "But we also don't have any intention of leaving them behind once the Drexian rescue arrives. The more we know about the prison and its weaknesses, the better chance we have for when the Drexian forces to pull off a mass break-out."

Fillian gave her a wide smile. "That sounds reasonable."

As he began to talk to us about the prison and what he remembered of the entrance and the security protocols and even the structure of the cavernous underground jail, I tried not to think of what Sam had told the Gatazoid.

She was right, of course. It made sense to wait until the Drexian forces arrived. If only we had any idea of when that would be. And if only we weren't living on borrowed time on a black moon that could kill us. For the hundredth time that day, I wished that Sam wasn't with me and that the thought of something bad happening to her didn't fill me with fear.

CHAPTER
TWENTY-ONE

Samaira

" I don't think he looks so great," I whispered to Jax, as I watched the Gatazoid waking up the next morning. We'd slept back-to-back after giving Fillian the cramped cave, neither one of us wanting to crowd in there with him.

I was eager to let the Gatazoid have the cave. I wasn't going to share it with Jax. Not after I'd woken up with him practically on top of me. Even now, thinking about being startled awake by the feel of his hard body pressing against mine and his hand over my mouth, my pulse fluttered, and my mouth went dry. It had been a long time since I'd been held by a man, and even though he'd only done it to keep me from making noise, the memory of his warm touch on my midriff and his soft breath on my neck was discomfiting.

I shouldn't have any reaction to Jax—and I absolutely

shouldn't feel a lurch in my stomach and a hot throb between my legs. He was the job. Nothing else. Still, most of my jobs didn't look like Jax.

"You don't like the way Gatazoids look?" Jax twisted around and frowned at me, a line forming between his eyes

In the light of day, I could see that Fillian's hair was a vibrant shade of purple, and his eyes were completely round. But it was the dusky circles under his eyes that worried me, not to mention the way the dingy prison jumpsuit hung off his skinny frame.

I swatted at the Drexian but kept my voice low as I turned fully around, stretching my legs and feeling the stiffness from spending hours sitting on hard rock. "That's not what I mean. I think the little guy looks ill."

Jax studied the alien as Fillian roused himself from where he'd curled up underneath the rock overhang. "He *has* been in a Kronock prison. I doubt any of their captives look great."

I nodded, agreeing with that. Even Jax looked sallow and wan after spending a few days in the Kronock brig, and I suspected Fillian had been in Kronock captivity for longer than that. I watched the way the Gatazoid's hand trembled as he rubbed his eyes. "He's weak. I doubt they feed them well in that prison. He probably needs to eat."

"We all need to eat," Jax muttered.

As if on cue, my stomach rumbled, and I pressed a hand to it. It had been over a day since I'd eaten, and my head was already aching from lack of food. I scanned the dense rainforest, wishing that it wasn't filled with poisonous plants and deadly creatures waiting to kill us.

Morning light sifted through the leafy treetops, sending slats of golden light to dapple the dark ground. The chirping sounds that had kept us company last night had been replaced by the caw of birds—at least, I hoped they were birds. After seeing the giant insect that made off with Jax's backpack and the long slithering one that tried to drop onto his shoulder, I wasn't eager to come face to face with more of the moon's native creatures.

Although there was abundant black foliage, I didn't spot anything creeping across the leaves. One thing about black moons where everything was poisonous—even creepy-crawlies couldn't survive if it was all toxic. I breathed in the humid air that was getting hotter and stickier by the second, the scent loamy and rich.

"If we can't forage anything to eat, we'll need to go back to the ship for rations," Jax said, as if he'd plucked the words from my head.

"What about the Kronock forces finding the ship?"

"It's a chance we'll have to take." He stood and stretched, his long arms brushing some low branches and his stomach muscles rippling. The Drexian hadn't put back on his environmental suit, even though it was dry. It seemed that he didn't mind walking around barely dressed.

When I saw Fillian's eyes widen, I laughed.

"What?" Jax looked down at me, his face a mask of innocent confusion.

"Do you ever plan on getting dressed again?"

He cut his gaze to the ripped fabric covering his crotch and little else. Then he met my eyes and his crinkled into a grin. "I'd heard that humans weren't comfortable with their bodies, but does mine bother you so much that you can't bear to look at it?"

My face warmed. It would have been wrong to say that I

couldn't bear to look at his hard body. Had a hard time not gaping at it was more accurate. "I didn't say it bothered me, but I'd think you'd want more coverage since we're in the middle of an alien death jungle."

"A hot alien death jungle," he corrected, letting his gaze slide down my body. "I'm surprised you haven't sweat through your clothing already."

I had, but I wasn't about to admit that to him. The form-fitting black pants and matching top that had seemed ideal for the mission were now blazing hot, and it wasn't even the heat of the day. I could only imagine how sweltering it would be once the sun hit the black leaves and inky undergrowth— and then my black outfit.

"The ship doesn't happen to stock extra clothing, does it?" I asked.

"Actually, there should be some standard issue Drexian garments."

I stood and brushed off the seat of my pants. "Then what are we waiting for?"

"Where are we going?" Fillian asked, his expression dazed.

I exchanged a look with Jax, and he handed the Gatazoid the water pouch. "You're staying here and getting some more rest while we go back to the ship we crashed in and get rations."

I jerked a thumb toward Jax. "And clothes for this guy."

Fillian giggled weakly at this before tipping the water into his mouth. He didn't drink much before handing it back to Jax. "Thank you."

Jax waved him off. "You keep it. We'll get more from the ship."

The little alien cradled the water pouch in his lap, his gaze darting nervously around him. "How long will you be gone?"

"We'll try to be as quick as we can," I said. "You should be able to stay hidden under the rock."

Glancing at the overhang, I realized that it wasn't a fool-proof hiding place during the day. At night, the shadows had hidden us, but there were no shadows now, and the cave didn't extend very far. Not to mention the fact that his purple hair was a shocking contrast to the black surroundings.

I stole another look at Fillian, whose cheeks were sunken and whose eyes drooped. He was in no state to tramp through the jungle and bringing him would only slow us down—or get us caught. We all stood a better chance if he waited for us and hid. Knowing all that didn't stop my gut from twisting at the thought of leaving him behind unguarded.

This is why you work alone, Sam. Others are a liability, especially if you care about them.

I might have just met the Gatazoid, but I did care what happened to him—and I hated that I did.

"You'll be fine," I told him, my voice gruffer than I'd intended it to be. "If you hear any noises, hide."

"And stay hydrated," Jax added.

Fillian bobbed his head up and down, but he nibbled at his lower lip as he watched us ready to depart.

I gave a brief scan of the area, committing it to memory so I could find my way back. Then I gave the Gatazoid a smile and a wave and turned sharply. Jax fell in step beside me as we walked quickly in the direction we'd come from.

"He'll be okay," he said, after we'd crunched through the undergrowth for long enough that Fillian couldn't hear us.

"I know," I snapped, then caught myself and huffed out a breath. "I'm not used to being responsible for anyone but myself."

"It's not always easy, is it?"

I cut my gaze to him to see if he was mocking me, but his expression was solemn. "No, it isn't. How do you do it?"

"Do what?"

"From what I gather, Drexians don't work alone. You're all about the unit. All for one and one for all, and all that bloody nonsense."

He held a slim branch up for me to pass under. "My Inferno Force brothers are the best thing about me."

"But you've lost them before, right? I mean, you can't be the toughest Drexians out there without suffering casualties."

He was quiet for a few seconds, and there were only the noises of the jungle and the crackling of the leaves under our feet. "I've lost brothers, but that doesn't shake my loyalty to Inferno Force. They're my family, and you don't abandon family."

My gut tightened as a pang went through me. Whatever family I had remaining had abandoned me long ago. Despite the many years that had passed, the feeling of rejection when my father had refused to bail me from jail the one time I'd called him was as fresh today as it had been when I'd been sixteen.

I shook it off. That was a lifetime ago, and I proved to myself that I didn't need him. I didn't need anyone. But the pang still throbbed like a dull ache in my heart. For all my eyerolling about the Drexians' smothering loyalty and obsessive-to-the-point-of-cocky honor, they had something I didn't.

I snuck a look at Jax. In all my years of stealing priceless baubles and breathtaking art, I was finally envious. He had something I ached for but could never allow myself to have.

TWENTY-TWO

Jaxon

I put my hand out to stop Sam when I spotted the shiny, black hull of the ship glinting through the trees. Even though it was black on black, the artificial shine was easy to spot in the daylight. "There it is."

We hadn't spoken for most of the trek through the thick rainforest. Sam had gone quiet after she'd asked me about losing Inferno Force brothers, and I couldn't tell if she was upset by my answer or confused. If I was being honest, the female was the most confusing creature I'd ever met. She was both aloof and caring, sometimes within the same breath. I could sense that she worried about the Gatazoid but was also unhappy and upset that she *had* to worry about him. This mission had clearly upended the way she usually worked, and she didn't know how to deal with it.

Sam went still immediately, her eyes the only thing

moving as she took in our environs. She'd even stopped breathing as she assessed the ship and the area surrounding it, reminding me again why she was so good at what she did.

"I don't hear anything," she whispered. "And there's no sign that others have been here. The only broken branches or flattened undergrowth are the ones along the path we made when we left."

I followed her gaze. She was right. We'd approached the ship from the same path we'd left it, and I didn't see evidence of any others. And if the burly Kronock had come through here, they would have left plenty of evidence.

"Just because they haven't been in the ship doesn't mean they might not be watching," I replied in my softest voice. "Or on their way."

"Then we need to get in there, get the goods, and get back to Fillian."

There was that concern again, her pretty lips pursed as she eyed me in challenge.

"Let's go," I told her, just as eager to get the job done as she was—and eager to eat.

I led the way to the ship, slipping in through the back hatch and holding out my hand to her. She didn't take it, instead climbing through on her own. And there was that maddening desire to do everything herself.

"I don't remember it looking this bad," she said in an almost reverent tone.

We stood at the back of the ship, the floor tilted from the awkward position in which the vessel had landed. The front view screen had been shattered, and green vines snaked in from above. My heart squeezed at the sight of the Drexian ship in such a state—and at the reminder that we wouldn't be getting off the alien moon in it.

The moist air had settled on every surface, making the glossy, black interior even shinier and the entire thing smell of mildew and something more fetid. My stomach roiled as I realized that what I was smelling was the bodies of my Drexian brothers. I put a hand over my mouth as bile teased the back of my throat.

"I guess we're lucky we weren't killed," Sam said, her usually warm complexion taking on a greenish hue as she glanced at the shiny body bags.

I pulled my own gaze away from them, shaking off my nausea and opening the nearest inset cabinet. "We should focus on getting supplies."

Sam didn't reply but took the pack I handed her and followed my lead, pressing her fingers on the smooth cabinet panels so that they popped open. I busied myself doing the same, filling my pack almost entirely with ration packs and pouches of water. I was so hungry I tore open one pouch, eagerly taking out the freeze-dried padwump and tearing off a chunk with my teeth.

"Here." I nudged Sam and handed her a piece.

She took a bite, making a face. "It's salty."

I opened a water pouch, handing that to her as well. "This should help."

After she took a long swig, she handed it back to me, and I gratefully drank. Once my hunger and thirst were taken care of, I returned to filling my pack. I jammed a pair of blasters in the top, twitching when something soft thudded against my bare back. Glancing down, I spotted a black

Drexian shirt and matching drawstring pants crumpled at my feet.

"In case you'd gotten your fill of parading around in your skivvies," Sam said without turning to meet my eyes.

I grunted in reply but picked them up. I wouldn't mind losing the filthy garment I'd worn since the day I was taken captive. I slid my boxer briefs off, stepping from them and picking up the drawstring pants.

"What in the bloody hell are you doing?"

Her shriek made me drop the pants and jerk my gaze to her. "I thought you wanted me to put them on."

Her eyes were wide as she made a point of keeping her gaze above my head. "I didn't know you'd be stripping down, first."

I sighed, almost amused by her shock. "You humans really do need to get over your sexual hang-ups."

"I don't have sexual hang-ups," she spluttered, her voice going up at least an octave.

I reached down and retrieved the pants I'd dropped, pulling them on and rearranging my cock while my gaze never left hers. "No? Then seeing me naked shouldn't bother you." I paused, tilting my head to one side. "Unless you've never been with—"

"Please." She cut me off with a roll of her eyes. "I'm not a virgin, if that's what you're asking, but I also don't date just anyone. And on Earth, men don't drop their pants like it's nothing."

I tugged the shirt over my head, aware that the twinge in my side wasn't as sharp as it had been a couple of days earlier. I was also aware of her gaze drifting to my muscles

SCORCH--A SCI-FI ALIEN WARRIOR ROMANCE

and then to the ink down my arm as I pulled the black fabric over my chest. "So, it's been a while."

She narrowed her eyes at me. "Not that it's any of your business."

I shrugged. "It isn't." Then I locked eyes with her, a familiar heat stirring in my core. "But it would be a shame if your policy about working alone extended to your personal life." I leaned closer to her. "It's never as much fun alone."

She reared back, her eyes flashing and her hand flying up. Before it could make contact with the side of my face, I caught her by the wrist.

Her chest was heaving as I pinned her arm around her back. "Let me go."

Before I could respond with something clever, a movement behind her drew my gaze. I jerked Sam toward me and away from the dark tentacles sliding down from above. Wrapping an arm around her and twisting so that my body shielded her, I snatched a blaster from the top of my bag and fired at the creature emerging from one of the cabinets.

With a shriek, it spasmed and fell, attempting to scuttle away as I continued to fire. I managed to blast off two of its many arms, finally hitting the bulbous head and killing it. Orange goo seeped from the creature as it twitched on the floor of the ship, the substance sizzling as it burned through the steel.

"Bloody hell!" Sam's chest heaved as she stared down at the corpse with my arm still snugly around her.

"More of the moon's natives," I muttered, steadying my breath and nudging the dark-skinned creature with one toe of my boot.

"This is the worst welcoming committee ever." Sam

made no move to pull away from me, if she'd even computed that I was holding her in the chaos. Then she peered up at me. "I guess I owe you one now."

"Considering how deadly this place is, we should probably stop keeping score."

She smiled at me before her eyes widened and she leaned away from me, as if suddenly aware of how close we were.

But I didn't want to stop holding her, and I pulled her back and lowered my head until my mouth hovered above hers. "I won't let anything hurt you."

Her breath hitched in her chest. "You can't make that promise. No one can."

I wanted to tell her that I would die before I let her be harmed, but a sound made me freeze. I used my other hand to cover her mouth as I listened again. Even Sam didn't move, no doubt recognizing the alarm in my eyes.

Even though it was still in the distance, something or someone was crashing loudly through the underbrush—and getting closer. When Sam heard it, she jerked in my grasp.

I released her wrist and mouth, putting a finger to my lips. From the speed at which the noises were approaching, we didn't have time to leave the ship. I looked desperately around the cramped and damaged cockpit, my gaze finally alighting on a narrow door. A slab of paneling had fallen and was blocking access to it, which made it the perfect—and only—place to hide.

Grabbing Sam's hand, I wiggled beneath the dangling panel and opened the door. The storage closet was barely big enough to hold the two of us, and I had to gingerly remove a few large tools before we could fit. I pushed Sam in first, and she flattened herself to one side, as the guttural sound of

Kronock voices reached us. Then I took a blaster from the top of my pack before joining the human female and closing the door silently behind us.

It hadn't occurred to me that it would be pitch black inside the closet as I stood body to body with Sam. I braced an arm on the wall over her head so I wouldn't crush her, since the angle of the ship made it so that she was tilted back, and I was pitched forward.

"Jax," she whispered, her breath tickling my neck as I bent over her.

Before she could say any more, heavy footsteps rocked the ship, jostling us both. The Kronock were inside the ship. I steadied my breath, counting my heartbeats and preparing myself to shoot if the door was opened.

Kronock curses were the first muffled words I heard, followed by, "I just stepped in dead Kurvian."

Now we knew what the tentacled creature was called.

"Careful or its guts will burn through your scales."

More cursing. "Drexians," a gravelly Kronock voice said.

"Dead Drexians," another added with a brutal laugh.

My body tensed at the thought of our despised enemy taking the bodies of my Drexian brothers. Sam pressed a calming hand to my chest, as if telling me not to react.

"You think they were attempting a rescue?"

A Kronock scoffed at this. "If they did, they failed."

"What do we do with them?"

There was shuffling and scraping. "Nothing. Let the jungle devour them. We have no use for Drexian corpses."

"They didn't put themselves in bags. Where are the others?"

There was a long pause as this realization settled over

the aliens. "They're probably dead too. Not many can survive on the black moon."

A grunt of agreement. "And the ship?"

"Do you want to have to drag this thing halfway across the moon?"

There were dark sounds of dissent.

"Then we don't mention it. The Drexians are dead. The ship is destroyed. The runaway isn't here. Why make more work for ourselves?"

Sam flinched at the mention of the runaway, but I rested a hand right below her throat, the rapid-fire beating of her heart vibrating up through my palm. We were so close I could feel every twitch of her muscles and every shallow breath. Once again, I was struck by how the feel of her fired my blood and sent need storming through me.

I rested my forehead on hers, steeling myself to her touch while also torturing myself. Any moment now the Kronock would leave, and my heart would stop hammering in my chest and my cock would stop aching.

"They got him," a Kronock voice called in from outside the ship, the sound more distant and garbled.

Sam inhaled sharply, but the Kronock didn't hear her over their own guffaws.

One of the Kronock inside barked out a cruel laugh. "That's it. Let's head back and help teach that little alien what happens when you run."

The ship jostled again as the Kronock stomped out, their voices receding into the jungle. When I finally opened the door, Sam was trembling from head to foot and tears streaked her face.

TWENTY-THREE

Samaira

"Come on." I cast a glance over my shoulder as Jax and I ran through the woods, the hanging ebony vines twisting around my arms and the sharp branches stinging my face. "It might not have been him."

We'd waited until we couldn't hear the Kronock before taking off in the direction of the small cave where we'd left Fillian, but I couldn't force myself to tread lightly. There was no time to waste, even though Jax's face when we'd emerged from the closet had told me that he believed the Kronock *had* been talking about Fillian.

But he hadn't protested when I'd started running away from the ship. Instead, he'd hoisted both packs onto his shoulders and followed closely behind me, his breaths heavy and his footfall a steady thud in my wake.

I lifted my hands to ward off some of the attacks from the jungle, lifting my knees high so they wouldn't get snagged on thick crawling vines that carpeted the ground. The sunlight was already sinking low on the horizon, which meant night was growing closer and the impending darkness would make it harder to find where we'd left Fillian. My vision was blurry, but I blinked hard to keep myself from crying again. I didn't have time for weakness now or for doubt.

It wasn't him, I repeated in my head. It wasn't him.

I couldn't handle losing another person I'd promised to keep safe, and I cursed myself for even allowing this to happen. I should have said no to the mission and told the Drexians they could shove their deal up their arse.

After running for a while longer, the sweat running down my back and settling in the waistband of my pants, we almost stumbled over the smooth, rocky ledge that formed the cave we'd camped in the night before. I pulled up fast, causing Jax to bump into me, grabbing my shoulders to keep from stumbling and taking us both down.

I shook off his hands and the uneasy reminder of how they'd felt on me back in the ship and the tingles that had sizzled over my skin when he'd been pressed up next to me. I didn't want to think about that now. I couldn't.

Dipping my head low, I peered into the open-mouthed cave. Nothing. Fillian wasn't there. I swiveled in place, scanning the area, and then tipping my head back to scour the treetops. "Fillian," I called, keeping my voice to an urgent whisper. "It's us. We're back. You can come out now."

There was no response.

I bent over and braced my hands on my knees, sucking in

air. Jax had been quiet, but he walked past me and scooped up the water pouch that lay on the ground. The cap was open, and a puddle of water had spilled out and collected on some shiny leaves.

Cold realization settled over me like a shroud, all the air in my lungs leaving me as if I'd been punched. Fillian wouldn't have run off without the water pouch, and he wouldn't have spilled any of the precious liquid. Not voluntarily.

I squeezed my eyes shut for a beat. Why was I so upset about an alien I barely knew? Fillian wasn't my friend. I'd barely known him. So why did I feel like I was losing Rayan again? Why did the same pain slam through me after all this time?

"Sam?" Jax's voice was soft, which made it even worse. If he'd been impatient or even cocky, I could snap back at him and take out some of my turmoil on him, but the git was being kind. Typical.

"They took him. We weren't here and they took him."

Jax dropped the two packs onto the ground. "We couldn't have known they'd find him. Leaving him was the only option. We all needed food and water, Fillian more than any of us. And you know he wasn't strong enough to make the trek to the ship."

I knew all of this, but it didn't make my failure any easier to swallow. I stood up and threw back my shoulders. "We have to go after him."

Jax eyed me like he was studying a wild animal. "I thought you didn't want to do anything rash. Didn't you argue for waiting for the Drexian rescue?"

I threw up my hands. "When will that be? By the time

your boys figure out where we are, the Kronock could have tortured Fillian to death."

I fingered the ring Vekron had given me, debating within myself if I should risk using it to speed up our rescue. But once I did, I'd be a walking beacon for the enemy as well—and useless in rescuing Fillian.

Jax flinched, something flitting across his eyes. "You're right. They won't be kind to an escaped prisoner."

"So, we break him out?"

Jax glanced around us, the shadows of the dark trees lengthening as the chirping of the nocturnal creatures began. "It will be harder to find the prison in the dark."

I thought back to what the Gatazoid had told us about the subterranean prison complex and how to reach it. "I remember the markers he described. I think I can get us there and get us in."

Jax bit his lower lip as he looked intensely at me. "This isn't like sneaking onto a Kronock battleship, and we won't have the luxury of arriving on a ship with stealth shielding."

I dropped to my knees and crawled into the cave, reaching my hand as far into the alcove as I could and retrieving the two environmental suits. "We have these."

"You hid them?"

I shook my head, giving a half shrug. "I balled them up to use as a pillow. That rock isn't the most comfortable thing to sleep on."

He took one of the suits from me, holding it in his hands and looking from it to me. "This is still dangerous, Sam. More dangerous than one of your cat-napping jobs."

Despite the fear and adrenaline coursing through my veins, I had to stifle a laugh. "Cat burglary." Then my mind went to Rayan lying in a slick pool of his own blood. "And trust me, they can be deadly."

He frowned. "If we get caught and the Kronock take you..." His voice cracked, and he tore his gaze from me.

"It would still be better than leaving Fillian to the Kronock."

He held my gaze for a moment, his eyes flashing, before he gave a rough shake of his head. "I shouldn't let you do this. You aren't trained. You aren't Drexian."

"Which is exactly why you can't prevent me from doing it," I said, curling my hands into fists. "I don't answer to you, Jax. I volunteered to come rescue you. I never signed up to take orders from you or any other cocky Drexian."

He closed the distance between us, looming over me as dusk fell over the moon. "I could make you stay."

I opened my mouth to argue with him, but he was right. He was so much bigger and stronger than me that if he wanted to, he could easily prevent me from doing just about anything.

Blood rushed in my ears as I reached up and fisted my hands in the fabric of his shirt, the sculpted muscles beneath my hands hard and unyielding. I needed him to let me go, and I needed him to get Fillian out. I couldn't do it alone, and for once, I didn't want to.

I peered up into his eyes, dark and molten with undisguised heat. I needed him—in so many ways I couldn't even process, the muddle of emotions roiling through me.

He gazed down at me, the breath stuttering in his chest, but he didn't move. Even when he shifted his gaze from mine to my lips and let out a low growl, he remained motionless.

"Please, Jax," I begged, the word feathering from my lips

moments before I yanked his head down and crushed his lips to mine.

CHAPTER
TWENTY-FOUR

Jaxon

I was so startled by Sam jerking my mouth to hers that I didn't react for a moment, my body stiff as she scraped one hand through my hair and held the back of my head tightly. Then the sensations of her lips—warm and soft and moving eagerly against mine—sent shockwaves racing along my spine. Heat pooled in my core, and my cock twitched as it strained against the fabric of my pants.

I didn't know what had made her throw herself at me—adrenaline, fear, the desire to prove she was still alive—but I could sense her need for me as if it were my own. And after everything that I'd been through, I needed to feel a connection as much as she did. I needed whatever she wanted me to give her. And when I thought about what I wanted to give her, desire pounded through me like a drumbeat for war.

With a possessive growl, I wrapped my arms around her

back, lifting her off the ground and walking her back until she bumped the stone ledge. My hands moved hungrily over her body, cupping her ass and lifting her up until she was sitting on top of the smooth ledge. The rock had been worn down so that the surface was smooth and the height was perfect for her to wrap her legs around my waist so that my hard cock pressed against her opening.

I groaned, grinding myself into her as I tipped her head back and delved deeper into her mouth. She moaned into my mouth, the sound desperate. Threading her fingers through my hair, she dug her nails into my flesh and arched into me with an insistent tug.

I was lightheaded as my tongue tangled with hers, the taste of her intoxicating. She was no shy female, her own tongue urgent as it stroked mine and explored my mouth without hesitation.

Scraping her nails down my neck to my shoulders, she tore her mouth from mine, her breaths ragged. Her dark eyes were hot and her voice smoky. "I want you."

My body buzzed with need, my shaft aching to be released. I cupped her jaw in one hand, locking my gaze on hers. "What do you want from me?"

Her eyelids lowered and she bit her bottom lip. "You know what I want."

I let out a low rumble, bending over her and running my lips up the length of her neck until my mouth brushed her earlobe. "Say it, Samaira."

She flinched at my use of her full name, jerking back and holding my gaze, her eyes narrowing slightly and her breath coming out in shallow bursts. "I want you to fuck me."

Molten heat fired inside me, sending frissons of pleasure

dancing across my skin. I attempted to steady my uneven breath as my gaze devoured her. "You want me inside you?"

She inhaled quickly, her lashes fluttering as her eyes rolled back in her head for a beat. "I don't want you inside me. I *need* you inside me. Right here. Right now."

Her hunger for me and the white-hot passion burning in her gaze made my knees nearly buckle. After a lifetime of practiced pleasurers with their rehearsed ecstasy and their contrived sounds, Sam's raw desire made me almost lose my ability to think.

I crushed my mouth to hers, my kisses hard and demanding. Dragging my hands down her body, I tugged at her shirt, pulling it from where it was tucked into her tight pants. When it was free, I jerked it up, breaking our kiss only long enough to pull it over her head.

I took in the sight of her round breasts, the edge of the dark nipples barely peeking from beneath the shiny white fabric. With a rough sound, I tugged the fabric aside from one hard nipple and set my mouth on it.

Sam moaned loudly, raking her fingers through my hair again as I sucked the tight point of her breast. When I nipped it lightly, she sucked in a sharp breath, coiling her legs around my back. Then I moved to the other breast, yanking the fabric aside and taking her pebbled flesh in my mouth.

I didn't know what I'd expected from a human female, but it hadn't been this. There was nothing quiet or reserved about Sam's reactions, and her loud gasps and groans only made me want to give her more pleasure. Reaching behind her back, I unfastened her bra and sat up, pulling the delicate garment off her body completely and gazing down at her.

Her nipples were hard and the brown flesh around them bumpy and moist from being sucked.

"Beautiful," I murmured, soaking up the sight of her soft mounds quivering as she heaved in breaths.

"Your turn," she said, nodding at my shirt, which I yanked over my head and tossed aside so fast she actually laughed. Then her gaze drifted down my chest, her pupils flaring. She leaned closer to me and dragged the tip of her tongue down one chest muscle, circling my nipple and finally giving it a hard nip.

I groaned, savoring the pain that quickly morphed into fiery pleasure. Then I pushed her back and grabbed the waistband of her black pants. "I wasn't done tasting you."

She licked her lower lip as she kicked off her shoes, putting her hands over mine and then using them to tug her pants down over her hips and her ass. I bent over and pulled them the rest of the way off, then hooked her legs over my shoulders. She yelped as she was thrust onto her back with her legs spread and my head between them.

"Jax," she said in a breathy voice, more a plea than anything. "I thought I told you I wanted you inside me."

I shook my head, eyeing the pretty glistening flesh that beckoned me. "Oh, you're going to get my cock, but not before I get you ready for me. This pretty pussy doesn't look like it can take all of me without a little work. You sure you want to take it?"

She gave me a wicked smile. "I can take anything you give me."

"That's my girl." I ran a finger through her folds and then slid it into my mouth. "But not before I make you come on my tongue."

She dropped her head back with a throaty moan of surrender, her legs falling open for me. With a ravenous growl, I ran my tongue through her slick folds until I found the little bundle of nerves I'd heard my Drexian brothers talk about. The Drexians who'd taken human mates spoke of the clit as magic, a way to bring release in human females that would make them nearly limp with pleasure.

As I swirled my tongue around the nub, Sam arched her back and grasped my shoulders. Loving her reaction and wanting more of her pleasure, I began flicking my tongue over it, my own cock a rigid bar. She clenched her legs around my head, her moans growing louder as I sucked harder. I'd never felt a female surrender to me completely like Sam was, her noises wild and needy. My desire to claim her body completely was almost uncontrollable, all rational thought replaced by raw need.

I slid one thick finger inside her, my cock aching to be sheathed by her tight heat. She gasped as I moved it in and out as I worked her clit.

"Jax." She tangled her hands through my hair as she knifed up, her legs trembling and her body bucking. It was all I could do to hold on as she gasped, her body clenching around my finger. When she slumped back onto the rock, her legs went limp over my shoulders, and her breaths shuddered in her chest.

I kissed the inside of her damp thighs and then straightened, savoring the look of the female as she moaned with pleasure. It was almost enough that I'd made her come so hard that her eyelids fluttered, and her chest heaved as if she'd run a race. Almost.

I tugged down my pants so that my cock sprang up, and I

dragged the swollen crown through her slickness, notching it at her tight entrance. I'd heard that human females were small for Drexian males, and that their pussies were tight for our cocks, but intoxicatingly so. I leaned over her, feathering a kiss along the hollow of her throat. "Have you ever been with a Drexian?"

She frowned through her haze. "You're my first."

That thought sent a possessive thrill through me. "You're my first human. I can go slow for you."

She blinked up at me, her gaze glinting with challenge. "Do I seem like the kind of woman who likes it soft and slow?"

Without answering, I scooped my arms around her back and drove my cock into her with a single hard stroke.

CHAPTER
TWENTY-FIVE

Samaira

I gasped as he entered me, the sudden intrusion making all the air leave my lungs. He paused once he'd filled me to the hilt, holding himself as my body adjusted.

Curling my arms around his back, my fingers slipped on his bare flesh that was slick with sweat. Between the heat of the alien jungle and the racing of my heart, I was burning up —and so was he. His skin was hot to the touch, my hands scorching as they gripped him.

When my fingers brushed the bumps running down his spine—hard and enflamed—my pulse quickened. These were the Drexian nodes I'd heard about, the nodules on their backs that signaled arousal. If his burning nodes were any indication, he was very aroused.

He hissed in a breath as my fingertips caressed the hard

bumps, then he touched his forehead to mine. "You're so *grekking* tight."

I managed to release a shaky breath. "You're so bloody huge."

His forehead furrowed, a rivulet of sweat trailing down the bumps. "Am I hurting you?"

"In a good way," I said. "I told you that I don't like it slow."

He dragged himself out slowly and then pushed back in, the stretch not burning as much. The muscles in his neck were strained, and his jaw ticked as he clearly fought to maintain control.

I moved my hands from his nodes and curled them so that my fingernails bit into his flesh. "I told you I like it hard, Jax." I dragged my nails down, scoring his skin with pink welts. "Hard and rough."

His eyes went black, and he opened his mouth in a silent roar, arching his back and thrusting deep inside me. He didn't hesitate as he reached back and grabbed my ankles, spreading my legs as wide as they could go and driving into me.

I moaned with each hard thrust, loving the feel of being filled by his thick cock and savoring the look of him as he pounded wildly into me, his long, dark hair falling into his face and his jaw clenched. His sculpted chest muscles were tensed, and his corded stomach rippled as he thrust into me, his rhythm savage.

His gaze raked my body as he lifted my ass off the rocks, his eyes locking on the place where our bodies joined and his expression dark and dominant—and surprised. "I didn't think your tight, little pussy would be able to take me."

"I told you I could take you," I said between stolen breaths, even though I'd never had a cock as big as Jax's, and it felt like he was splitting me in two, but in the best way possible.

"You did," he gritted out, his eyes flaring hungrily. "I'm buried inside you."

I propped myself up on my elbows, gazing down at where he split me. There was something so hot about watching his long, thick cock thrusting inside me and knowing that I was taking every inch of him.

"You like watching me fuck you?" he husked out, his gaze meeting mine.

I nodded, pulling my bottom lip up in my teeth. Then I put a finger in my mouth, dragging it out and sliding it down to my clit. "Do you like watching this?"

Jax lost his rhythm for a second as he watched me circle my finger around my swollen nub, his gaze dark and intense. It didn't take long for the sensations to storm through me and for my body to start clenching around him.

"Come for me," he said, his words more of a command as he stroked deep and put his own fingers over mine, moving them in unison.

I let out a silent gasp, clenching his hand and pressing it to my clit as my release left my legs shaking. The only noise that came from him was a stifled snarl as he pulled from me and flipped me over, bending me at the waist. I braced my hands on the rocks as he bent his legs and grasped my hips, tilting my ass up to give him better access.

"Such a pretty ass," he groaned, grabbing one ass cheek and squeezing it. "Almost as pretty as your pussy."

I twisted my head to look at him, his massive cock

standing out ramrod straight from his body. I twitched my ass at him. "You aren't done fucking me, are you?"

He gave me a crooked smile, then slapped my ass with one open palm. "That's for being impatient."

"Ow!" I jerked, but he was holding my hips tight.

"I thought you said you could handle anything I gave you."

I wiggled in his grasp. "Just because you're bigger than me, doesn't mean—"

He bent over and lowered himself, spreading my legs with his knee and burying his cock inside me. "Doesn't mean what?"

I couldn't help letting out a moan of pleasure as the new angle went even deeper.

"That I can do what I want with your perfect little body and fuck you until you scream? I thought that's what you wanted, Samaira." He started stroking his cock in and out, as he leaned over my back, his words sending heat simmering over my flesh. "You wanted me to claim your body as my own and show you what it's like to be fucked by a Drexian warrior, didn't you?"

Even as my legs wobbled and my eyes fluttered, I fought to snap back a response to the cocky alien. "You're fucking me so good, maybe I'll have to try more Drexians. See if the rest of them can fill me like you do."

It was a flirty lie meant to tease him, but Jax growled loudly in response, running his hand up into my hair and fisting it around my locks. He pulled my head back so that it was flush with his, and his lips buzzed my ears. "You're mine. No other Drexian can have you."

I hated arrogant guys, and possessive ones even more,

but for some reason, his dominant words excited me. It had been so long since anyone had called me theirs that I hungered for the feeling of being possessed, even if it was by a cocky alien like Jax.

Still, I tilted my head, so my breath feathered across his lips. "Prove it. Mark me as yours, Jax." I hesitated for only a second. "I want you to come inside me."

With a jerk, he knifed up, hammering deep inside me before throwing back his head and pulsing hot into me. We were both panting when he slumped over me, holding his own hands on either side of me so he wouldn't crush me with his weight as his scruffy cheeks scratched my back.

Slowly, the sounds of the jungle came back to me, the chirping of alien creatures blending with our heavy breathing. As the euphoric haze faded and the reality of our situation rushed back in, I closed my eyes and tried to steady my breath. The huge alien was still inside me, his cock still hard, and a part of me knew I'd miss the feeling, although I had no doubt I'd be sore for days. The other part of me wondered what the bloody hell I'd just done.

CHAPTER
TWENTY-SIX

Jaxon

"Samaira," I said, as she gathered her clothes from the glittering, black rock. She ignored me as she shook them out and started to get dressed again, pulling her panties on first. "Sam!"

My sharp tone made her swivel her head to me and pause with one pant leg halfway up her calf. "What?"

Now that I'd gotten her attention, I wasn't sure what I wanted to say. Almost as soon as we'd both started breathing normally and I'd pulled out, Sam had started bustling around the site for her clothes. She hadn't said anything or turned to look at me. I suppose I hadn't been expecting her to fall into my arms or insist I hold her, but I'd expected more than this. Even the pleasurers I'd paid handsomely for their time and manufactured affection had been less eager to leave my embrace.

"What is it, Jax?" Even through the dusk, the whites of her eyes shone.

"Why are you...?" Pretending like nothing just happened, I felt like saying, but instead I picked up her silky bra and handed it to her. "In such a rush?"

She took the bra from me, her fingertips brushing across mine and sending a tingle up my arm. "Nothing has changed, has it? We're still going to break Fillian from the Kronock prison, aren't we?"

"Yes," I said, leaning my bare ass against the smooth rock overhang and making no move to get dressed myself. "But we can catch our breath first."

She tugged her pants over the ass I'd smacked not long ago, fastening them at her waist and straightening. "I didn't think Drexians would need more recovery time than humans."

I frowned at this, but she was still topless, and it was hard to be irritated with her and stare at her magnificent breasts at the same time without my mind wandering back to having my mouth on them and the feel of her velvety-soft skin on my lips. "We don't but shouldn't we talk about—?"

She huffed out a breath and closed the distance between us. "I really didn't expect big, tough Inferno Force warriors to be the type to want to talk through everything." She pressed a palm against my sweaty chest. "We both needed to burn off some aggression and energy, so we did. It was fun, but that's all it was. A bit of fun."

I eyed her. Since when did females—paid pleasures aside —talk like this?

"Do you still plan to return to Inferno Force?" she asked.

"Of course," I answered, before even thinking about it.

"And I still plan to go back to Earth." She patted my chest. "Nothing's changed for either of us, which is the way it should be." She leaned in close to my ear. "Not that I wouldn't mind a repeat performance before I go home."

I gaped at her as she turned and resumed dressing, while humming to herself. Maybe I should be pleased that she'd enjoyed our encounter and wasn't behaving like a clingy female, but I'd expected a bit more attachment than this. My gut clenched as I fought the feeling of rejection that threatened to morph into anger. This was why I hadn't wanted to get involved with the human. She'd seemed different, but maybe she was just as dangerous as the tribute who'd rejected me, although in this case Sam *did* know me so her attitude hurt more, if that was possible.

Then I gave my head a rough shake. You do everything in your life to avoid getting tied down, a little voice in the back of my head reminded me. You don't want a female of your own, and the last thing you want is a human bride. Not anymore.

This was all true, but why did I feel a sting as I watched her so easily shake off the fact that I'd been balls-deep inside her only minutes ago? Why did her ability to switch gears feel like a fresh betrayal?

"Jax?"

Her voice snapped me from my mental wanderings and made the voice in my head vanish. I peered at her through the encroaching darkness.

She flapped a hand at me, her gaze darting to my naked body, lingering for a beat on the cock that was now hanging between my legs. "Are you going to get dressed or is this part of your strategy to distract the Kronock?"

"I doubt this would distract them." I straightened and snatched my own pants from the ground, catching her eyes and giving her a half smile. "It might distract you."

She pulled her eyes from me, tugging her shirt on over her head. "You've already distracted me enough for one night."

Once I'd put on my pants, I reached for her arm and pulled her to me, needing to prove to myself that she did want me. "I could distract you some more. Drexians actually don't need time to recover."

She swatted me, but her pupils were still flared. "Nice try, Romeo, but we need to get to that prison."

"Jax," I corrected, anger flashing through me. Who was Romeo?

A giggle escaped Sam's lips. "I know your name. Romeo is a character in a play from Earth. A famous lover and sweet talker."

I grinned, our banter weakening my doubts. "You can call me a great lover any day."

She rolled her eyes. "I didn't. Romeo was only a kid. I doubt he was any good at all. Luckily for him, Juliette was even younger and had nothing to compare him to."

I scowled at this. Maybe I didn't want to be compared to the Romeo, after all.

Sam put her hands on my chest. "You were great. Ten out of ten. Now can we go break Fillian from the Kronock jail?"

One thing I understood was the desire to save a friend or brother. "We need a plan."

She huffed out a breath but nodded. "So, what's the plan? You know the Kronock better than I do."

"From what Fillian told us, the prison is not far in that

direction." I jerked my head behind me, then I plucked my shirt from the ground and yanked it over my head. "The entrance isn't hidden, but it's flush with the ground."

"There aren't guards up top, but there is a security panel that requires a code. I'll be able to hack into that."

After Sam had managed to get through the Kronock battleship and open my cell, I didn't doubt her breaking and entering skills. "We'll need to move fast. Once the enemy knows we're there, we won't have much time." And we'll be trapped underground, I thought but didn't say. Sam might not mind enclosed spaces like vent shafts, but the thought of descending into an underground prison sent tremors through me.

"Fillian said the cells themselves and all the gates leading from level to level are controlled by a central computer. Once I override that, we should be able to move freely through the subterranean complex."

I picked up one of the packs I'd filled at the ship and unzipped it, handing her a blaster. "You'll need this."

Even though there was little light spilling through the dark treetops, Sam's hesitation was noticeable.

"You do know how to fire one, don't you?" I asked, holding it out in my open palm.

"I guess there's no hoping it won't come to violence, is there?"

I studied her, curious that a woman who'd chosen a life of crime didn't embrace violence. "Not when it comes to the Kronock. If they see us, they'll fire. We have to be prepared to defend ourselves—and Fillian."

Her lips flattened into a tight line as she took the blaster from me and tucked it into the back of her pants.

"I hope you don't shoot off that pretty little ass of yours."

The hard line of her lips softened as she smirked at me. "I did get a crash course in blaster use from your captain. There's a safety. But thanks for the compliment on my ass."

"Anytime." I was glad I'd lightened the mood, although thinking of her ass did make my cock stir, and I shifted my stance.

"Fillian told us his cell was on the third level down with the other political prisoners who're considered non-violent and not a threat," Sam said. "If they took him back to his old cell."

I pulled the environmental suits from the bottom of one of the packs, assessing the fabric that now appeared dull in patches. "These might have been damaged by the mud we jumped in, but they're still our best bet for moving unnoticed through the prison."

Sam sighed even as she took her old suit from me. "I hope Fillian appreciates the sacrifice of me dripping with sweat in this thing."

Unless our plan—what little there was of it—went off perfectly, we'd be sacrificing a lot more than sweat for this mission. There was a decent chance one or both of us wouldn't make it out. One human and one Drexian against a prison filled with Kronock were not great odds.

We both stepped into the suits, fastening them all the way up to our necks but leaving the hoods off.

"This is not going to make it easy to sleep," I muttered.

She snapped her head to me. "Sleep?"

I put my hands over hers, pressing her fingers to the bare flesh of my chest, which had yet to return to its normal pace.

"If it's one thing I know it's that rushing into battle is a mistake."

She jerked back from me. "What?"

I gestured around us. "We need to wait until there's some light. This place is dangerous enough as it is. If we go stumbling through the dark, we might overshoot the prison."

She opened her mouth to argue, but I shook my head forcefully. "No arguments, Sam. We wait until light—what there is of it. Until then, we get some rest."

Her eyes narrowed for a moment before she shrugged. "Fine, but not a second after first light." She sat down on the rock, putting the blaster beside her, and lay back with her hands laced behind her head, glancing up at me. "If I'm going to sleep, you'd better too."

I released a breath, grateful she wasn't forcing me to argue with her about my decision, but not thrilled by her sharp tone. We'd gone from fucking to fighting, and I much preferred the fucking.

"I'll keep watch for a while."

"Suit yourself," she grumbled, "but don't blame me if you're tired for our mission."

Sitting down next to her, I wrapped my arms around my bent knees and leaned back against the rock ledge. Part of me wanted to lie next to her, but I could tell from her body language that she was irritated with me, so I closed my eyes and listened to the comforting cadence of her breath, hoping rest would temper her anger.

CHAPTER
TWENTY-SEVEN

Jaxon

I don't know what woke me from my sleep—or when I'd fallen asleep—but it was still night when my eyes flew open. The chirping of the birds and scuttling of insects hadn't grown louder, but something had changed. I stiffened as I listened for the sound of approaching Kronock, but there was nothing. My body relaxed as I recognized the familiar rainforest sounds and nothing more. Then I turned to glance at Samaira.

Grek.

I leapt to my feet when I saw the empty rock beside me. The space where she'd been sleeping was empty, and a quick peek under the ledge confirmed that she wasn't there.

"Treacherous female," I growled, curling my hands into fists. She'd pretended to go along with my plan, waited until

I'd fallen asleep, and then snuck out on her own. I wasn't sure if I was terrified or livid.

I tipped my head up to the sky and fought the urge to bellow my frustration. Had everything been a lie? Had she fucked me to get me to do what she wanted? Had she faked her pleasure? Had she faked all of it?

Bile rose in the back of my throat, sharp and bitter. How had I let myself trust another human female? Hadn't I learned better than to give them any power over me?

I cursed under my breath as I scanned the dark rainforest. How could she be so foolish to run off by herself? She knew how deadly the planet could be. I caught sight of the packs on the ground. She hadn't even taken supplies, which made my stomach roil.

"What was she thinking?"

She was thinking that she had to save Fillian, I reminded myself. I clearly hadn't understood how driven she was to rescue him and how tormented she was by the thought of losing someone else. Regret twinged inside me, edging out some of my rage.

It didn't matter, I told myself. She'd still betrayed me and abandoned me, the all too familiar feelings consuming me even as I scooped up the packs and stormed off in the direction Fillian had indicated. As much as I wanted nothing more to do with yet another woman who'd hurt me, I also couldn't let anything happen to her. Not only because I was Drexian, and she was my responsibility but because I cared for her. I hated myself for it, but the thought of her being in danger made me tear through the jungle even faster.

I hadn't been running long when I caught a glimpse of movement to one side. I stopped, peering through the vine-laden trees, and could make out a face bobbing along as if levitating in mid-air.

"Samaira!" I didn't bother to keep my voice low as I yelled out to her.

She stopped and pivoted to face me. "Did I wake you when I left?"

Her voice was so casual that it stoked my rage even hotter. I thrashed over and loomed over her, grabbing her arm and jerking her body flush to mine. "What the *grek* do you think you're doing?"

"Saving Fillian. I told you I couldn't risk him being killed."

"And I told you we'd go together in the daylight." My body shook with anger, but she didn't cower from me.

"I'm sorry, Jax, but I couldn't wait." Her jaw was tight. "I can't lose anyone else."

"Sorry?" I gaped at her. "You left me. I didn't know what had happened. I didn't know..." My voice cracked. "Was any of it real, or was it all part of your con?"

She cocked her head at me. "What con?"

"You deceive for a profession, right?" I waved a hand between us. "This. Was fucking me part of your plan? Something to distract me?"

She recoiled. "No. Is that what you think?"

I released her and staggered back. "I don't know what to think. All I know is that you lied to me, and you left me. In all your panic about losing Fillian, did you even care about losing me?"

Her mouth fell open. "Jax, I didn't think—"

A weight was compressing my chest, the air coming out of me in desperate snatches of breath and making my voice low and gruff. "It doesn't matter. You want to save Fillian? Let's save him."

She stepped closer to me, holding out her hand. "Jax—"

I shook my head. "I won't let you go in alone, but once we're done with this mission, that's it, Sam. I don't want to be involved with a female who deceives so easily."

She jerked back as if I'd struck her but then she pressed her lips together, nodding. "If that's the way you want it."

My chest ached so much I wondered if I was dying, but I forced the words out. "It is."

"Okay then." Sam slid a silver ring off her finger and looked at it. "I guess now's the time to activate this thing. We've got nothing left to lose, right?"

"What thing?" I peered at the innocuous shiny band.

"Your friend Vekron gave this to me before I left." She met my gaze. "It's a beacon so the Drexians can find us."

CHAPTER
TWENTY-EIGHT

Samaira

His mouth dropped as he swiveled his head between me and the ring resting in my hand. "A beacon? And you're just telling me about this now?"

So much for calming him down. "If I'd activated it any earlier, it would have alerted the Kronock that we were here and brought a fleet of them down on our heads. Is that what you wanted?"

He scowled at me, silent for a moment. "Then why activate it now?"

I wasn't sure how precise the beacon was, or if the Kronock could easily detect it, so my plan could be a total fail. "If we leave it here, it might draw the enemy away from the prison. While they're here, searching for the source of the Drexian beacon, we'll be breaking into their prison and enjoying the advantage of fewer guards."

"This has been your plan all along?"

"No," I admitted. "But I knew I couldn't activate the beacon until the last possible moment. The moon isn't huge. Once they know we're here and calling for Drexian backup, it won't be long until they hunt us down."

"You really do have the mind of a criminal."

It didn't sound like a compliment, but I decided not to be offended. I already knew what he thought of me. "Or a military strategist. Same difference."

Jax grunted, scooping the ring into his palm. "Is it activated?"

I reached over and twisted it three times while pressing on the sides. "Now it is."

"Then we shouldn't make it so easy for them to find the source of the beacon." He threw the ring into the dense jungle. "That should keep them busy."

"No going back now." I took the pack he handed me and hoisted it on my back.

His eyes locked on mine, but the intensity was different this time. "No going back."

I wanted to try to explain myself again, but he turned quickly and started walking, so I followed. I hated that he was so angry with me, but we'd never been anything but a bit of fun, right? Neither of us had ever wanted more, and we both had enough baggage to fill the boot of a car. It was better this way.

I sighed, blinking away stinging tears. Then why did I feel like rubbish?

We tramped silently through the shadowy forest, him staying slightly in front of me, and not looking back. After a while, he reached back and grabbed my hand without a word.

When I attempted to tug it away, startled by the sudden touch, he clamped on tighter. "If you decide to go plunging into a mud hole again or make a run for it, I want to know."

"Jax, listen—"

He wheeled around, a muscle ticking in his clenched jaw, but we were interrupted by the crashing noises coming toward us. We both knew exactly what it was without speaking, and he pulled me down into the thick underbrush as the Kronock guards barreled by us.

They were far enough away for us to be easily masked by our suits and the blackness of the surroundings, but I still held my breath.

"How much farther?" one of the Kronock asked.

"Up ahead."

"You think it's from the Drexian ship?"

"What Drexian ship?"

There were dark mumblings as the enemy guards tramped on, arguing with each other as the one guard stammered out excuses. When the voices had faded, and the heavy footfall no longer shook the ground beneath our feet, Jax stood, pulling me up beside him.

"At least we know we're on the right track," I whispered.

He didn't respond, but moved forward even faster, ducking under tree branches and around dark trunks with bark peeling off in large curls. The faint light from overhead drifted through the heavy umbrella of leaves, but it was enough light for Jax to follow the path the Kronock had made from their thick tails flattening the underbrush and snapping branches off trees.

I tipped my head back, wondering if the Drexian were above us somewhere, their fleet massing in Kronock space as a response to our beacon. Or were we too far away for the subspace frequency to reach them, despite what Vekron had said?

I wasn't used to relying on backup from anyone. My jobs were solo missions. If I got caught, I got caught. Me alone. No one would be coming in to rescue me, but no one would pay for my mistakes, either. It was why I planned my jobs so precisely, rehearsing them and doing so much reconnaissance that by the time I pulled the job, it was almost anticlimactic.

Which was why my racing heart and tight throat were unfamiliar sensations to me. This plan had been thrown together and had limited chances of success. If I were back on Earth, I never would have attempted something so reckless especially with a partner.

Jax might have been a tough Drexian, but that didn't make me feel any less responsible for him. My mission had been to get him *away* from the Kronock, not drag him back into their lair. But I also couldn't leave Fillian to a life of imprisonment. Not when he'd trusted us to get him off the black moon.

I focused on the back of Jax's head as I followed him. It was the only part of him that wasn't masked by the environmental suit's stealth shielding, his long hair spilling over the scrunched hood at the back of his neck. My stomach churned as I thought about fisting my hands in his hair and then of that same hair flopping in his face as he'd thrust deep inside me.

It had always been a hard and fast rule to never pull a job with someone I'd slept with. It hadn't been a tough one to keep since I worked alone, but even when I didn't, most of the guys in my line of work didn't appeal in the least. But here I was, preparing to attempt the most dangerous job of my life with Jax's seed still trickling down my leg.

I closed my eyes for a second, attempting to purge my mind of thoughts of him. I needed to focus on the job—not on how amazing he'd felt inside me. Especially since he'd made it clear he didn't want anything to do with me once we'd gotten off the moon.

Get it together, Samaira, I told myself. Even I used my full name when I meant business. *It's over. Besides, it was never meant to be. Relationships weren't in the cards for you. They never have been. Not real ones, at least.*

Jax slowed in front of me, coming to a stop and dropping my hand so he could hold me back with one arm.

I leaned around him to see. "What is it?"

The tangled vines crawling across the ground had given way to a wide expanse of shiny metal that glinted in the scant light. Even though it wasn't a small entrance, it was inset in the ground and would be easy to miss if we'd been walking twenty feet in either direction.

"Where's the access panel?" I whispered as I squinted through the darkness.

Jax put a finger to his lips and knelt, moving his hands around the edge of the flat hatch. I followed his lead, moving in the other direction, my fingers skimming the smooth steel.

The entrance was a rectangle with a bar running along one side, presumably to hoist the door manually once it was unlocked. It was hard to imagine that there was an entire subterranean prison running underneath this unassuming entrance. No noises came through the ground or any other indication of what was being hidden beneath the moon's surface. The thought of hundreds of creatures being held in cells right under my feet made a shiver skate down my spine.

"Here," Jax whispered from the other side of the long handle.

I made my way to him, kneeling so that our knees brushed. The panel was flush to the metal at the corner, wide buttons emblazoned with unfamiliar symbols.

"Kronock letters," he said, his voice thick with disdain.

Unzipping my environmental suit, I reached into the snug pocket of my pants and retrieved a flat device, attaching it to the panel and saying a prayer that it would still work after being submerged and knocked around plenty. "It doesn't matter. Machines are machines."

Within moments, the device whirred to life, tapping into the rudimentary panel lock and deciphering the code, which flashed on the small screen. I blew out a relieved breath.

Jax swung his head to me. "That's it?"

"I'm guessing this prison has been here for a while, and the Kronock haven't upgraded to anything more sophisticated." I removed the device and slipped it back in my pocket before punching in the code. "We got lucky."

The panel blinked blue and there was a clicking noise. Jax grabbed the handle and jerked it up, the heavy metal door lifting slightly. "We're about to crawl into the ground with who knows how many Kronock. Lucky isn't the word I'd use."

I drew in a shaky breath, savoring the warm, jungle air as I got a whiff of the dank, loamy air emerging from underground. I hated that Jax was right.

CHAPTER
TWENTY-NINE

Jaxon

Despite the fabric covering my skin, bumps prickled my arms as I inhaled the cold, fetid air wafting up from below. I braced my legs on the steel edge of the entrance as I held the door open for Sam, fear gripping my chest as she descended the steep steps leading into the enemy's subterranean domain. I might be furious with her, but that didn't stop me from being scared for her.

Once she was in, I stole a final breath of the sticky air above ground. I never thought I'd miss the humid heat of the black moon's jungle, but anything was better than the dankness of the Kronock underworld. Stepping quietly behind Sam, I pulled the door closed on top of me, the sharp click making my gut tighten into a hard ball.

As soon as we were inside, sounds drifted up from below

—wails, scream, bellows. Some I recognized as guttural Kronock voices, but others were clearly alien. My hackles rose along with the tang of bile in the back of my throat. How many innocent creatures were being held by the cruel and unforgiving Kronock?

If I'd thought it was dark on the surface of the black moon, the underground prison was shrouded in even more darkness, with no faint moonlight to creep between ebony leaves. Orbs of green ambient light were embedded in the walls but spaced far enough apart that I had to narrow my eyes through the green glow to track Sam's hair as she crept down the staircase.

Leaning over the metal steps, I could make out that they spiraled down so far I couldn't see where they ended. I gulped. How far had the Kronock burrowed into the earth, and how many aliens were trapped beneath tons of earth and steel?

I was so preoccupied that I didn't notice that Sam had stopped, and I bumped into her, sending us both against one of the cold stair railings. My body cocooned hers for a moment, and the heat sent a comforting pulse through me.

She elbowed me in the ribs, pointing to another panel in the dirt wall, this one at a wider landing below. It held a screen, and no buttons or Kronock symbols.

"Maybe it's the system panel," she whispered, moving quickly to it.

Even if it was, I didn't know how she expected to get access, but I followed her, noticing that the landing extended in both directions, with gates blocking access to the corridors carved into the rock and dirt.

Sam was focused entirely on the panel that was at

Kronock eye level, so her head was tipped up as she studied it. She was so deeply in the zone that she must not have heard the rhythmic tapping of metal against metal coming from one side.

Swiveling my head to the sound, my heart lurched, and my body stiffened. A Kronock guard in a helmet that encased the top half of his head strode lazily down one of the corridors, dragging his metal baton across the bars of what I now saw were cells. He was facing away from us, but I could tell that he'd soon turn.

Without thinking, I flipped up my hood to cover the back of my head and pressed myself against Sam, encasing her body with my own and covering her exposed head. She twisted her head up to complain but I covered her mouth with my own, swallowing her arguments. Even though she emitted a squeak of protest, that noise was muffled by the bulk of my body and my lips locked on hers. I held my body against her mercilessly, even though she wiggled, her movements making it hard to maintain focus and not become aroused. I hated how good she felt, how much I'd longed for her touch, and how right she felt with me.

The metallic pings didn't change their pace, growing closer to us. I didn't dare look over or release Sam. Not when the only thing hiding us from the Kronock was my body covered by the environmental suit's stealth shielding.

The sharp sounds paused, and the Kronock let out a grunt. "Anyone there? Krokot, that you?"

Sam stilled beneath me, her mouth becoming pliant as the Kronock dragged in wet breaths so close to us I was sure I could feel the heat of him. Then he walked away with a snort, dragging his baton down the cell bars again.

I released Sam, whose eyes were wide. She blinked up at me, her expression questioning and hopeful before realization dawned on her, and she darted a momentary glance around my arm at the alien guard before quickly masking her disappointment and turning back to the panel. Her fingers swiped expertly through multiple screens that appeared to be a map of the complex. I clenched my jaw when I saw how expansive the prison was, and how many cells it contained. After a few swift taps, there was a series of clicks that echoed around us and from below. She'd unlocked something. I only hoped it was the right something.

Sam gave me another pointed look, jerking her head toward the stairs. I heaved in a breath. I was still blocking her body from being seen by the guard, but as soon as we moved, she'd be revealed. Very slowly, I slipped one hand up her body and lifted her hood over her hair.

I was tracking the guard's footfall, and when he reached the gate separating us and turned around to walk back the other way, I made a dash for the stairs and pulled Sam behind me.

When we were halfway down the winding stairs, I paused. She was still one step above me, so I tugged her head to mine, whispering into her ear. "If that was the first level of cells, Fillian should be two levels down."

She nodded. "I unlocked the gates to the cell blocks. I think."

We'd find out soon enough, I thought, as I continued spiraling down the stairs, being careful to walk on my toes so the metal wouldn't rattle. When we reached what should have been the third level I hesitated before stepping onto the landing. There was no sound of a guard banging his baton on the cell bars, but that didn't mean there was no guard.

I pulled out my blaster, glancing back at Sam. "Ready?" I mouthed.

She gave me a look of determination that I couldn't help but admire. The female was brave, I'd give her that. Or incredibly foolish. I hadn't yet decided.

I descended to the landing, pivoting my head to take in both sides of the corridor. There was a Kronock guard, but he was leaning against the wall with his arms crossed. Sleeping, I thought with a rush of satisfaction.

I didn't wait for him to wake and sound an alarm, leveling my blaster and firing at his chest. Sam jumped beside me but didn't hesitate to move through the now unlocked gate. Luckily, the noise of the blaster was masked by random bellowing throughout the prison, and no one reacted to the sound. I suspected blaster fire wasn't unheard of within the prison. We both walked hurriedly down the row of cells, stepping over the Kronock slumped dead on the floor, and peering into the small dark rooms fronted by iron bars. Shocked faces returned our gazes, the expressions going from surprised to relieved.

At the end of the row, Sam sucked in a breath. "Fillian!"

The Gatzoid was huddled in the corner, his skinny arms wrapped around his bent legs. He jerked his head up, his eyes growing even rounder than normal. Sam didn't waste any time pulling the device from her pants pocket again and working it in the old lock mechanism. Just like it had when Sam had rescued me from the Kronock battleship, the cell door swung open.

Sam rushed inside and helped him up while I swung my

head toward the stairs, hoping that the sounds of the blaster and then the opening of a cell hadn't alerted any of the other Kronock.

"You came!" Fillian's high voiced cracked as he spoke, which was a good thing since we didn't need any more noise.

I put a hand under the alien's armpit and bustled him from the cell. "We don't have time to talk now. We still need to get you out."

Fillian's eyes went to the other cells and the occupants who'd now rushed to the bars. I recognized a Neebix, his curly hair matted and his tail drooping on the ground, and an Allurian, his light-green skin pallid. My stomach roiled at the sight of these aliens, all from planets we'd liberated from the Kronock.

I shook my head. "We can't leave them."

Sam glanced at the aliens clutching the bars, her gaze going to the locks. "How long do I have to unlock all of these?"

A loud thud sounded from above us, followed by a roar. "Who opened these gates?"

"Not long," I told her, readjusting my grip on my blaster as heavy footsteps rattled the staircase overhead. From the sounds of it, an entire herd of Kronock was descending on us.

THIRTY

Samaira

I'd rarely had to open so many locks and never under the pressure of an approaching horde of violent aliens. I took a second to take a breath then squared my shoulders and approached the nearest cell where a creature with pale-pink skin and bobbling feelers extending from her forehead stared at me with pleading eyes. "I'd better crack on."

Before I could start work on the lock, Fillian grabbed my arm. "You can open them all from the master panel."

I glanced at the panel at the base of the stairs. "The cells are controlled centrally?"

He bobbed his head up and down. "They don't use it often, but I heard the guards talk about it once. If they ever had to clear the prison, they could open them at the same time."

I exchanged a glance with Jax. The panel was at the base of the stairs—the stairs the Kronock were currently thundering down.

"Go," he said, his jaw tight. "I'll cover you."

I didn't stop to think about how dangerous it was, or that I'd have my back to the onslaught. One look at Jax told me that he'd defend me with his dying breath. I only hoped it wouldn't come to that.

I reached the panel with Jax on my heels. He squared off with his blaster in front of him while I concentrated on the panel. Swiping my fingers across the smooth surface, I ignored all the Kronock symbols that popped up. When it came down to it, hacking was the same despite language differences, and once I was searching for it, it was easy to find the cell controls on the schematics. I got into the central locking mechanism as the sound of blaster fire erupted behind me.

Kronock screams filled the air along with the thud of heavy bodies falling down the stairs. Jax backed up until his body touched mine. Instead of bothering me, his touch was comforting, reminding me that he literally had my back. It had been a long time since anyone but me had had my back.

More footsteps rocked the stairs, rattled and shaking the platform I was standing on as Kronock reinforcements swarmed from both below and above. I didn't look away from the screen, but felt Jax swing his blaster up and down, laser fire volleying around us. Focusing fully on the job at hand, I tapped quickly and disarmed the locking mechanisms on all levels.

Even though the sounds of the cell lock disengaging were

masked by the noise of the battle, I knew it had worked when the aliens from the adjoining corridors spilled out.

"The cells are open!" Fillian screamed, his high-pitched voice no longer weak and thready.

From deep within the underground prison, cheers erupted, followed by more roars from Kronock guards.

I spun around. Jax was firing at the Kronock as they appeared from both directions of the stairs. Since he was in his environmental suit, only the front of his face was visible, making him a much smaller target. I suspected the Kronock didn't have time to figure out where the blaster fire was coming from before they were cut down.

"We've got to get out," I yelled over the rising cacophony of prisoner screams, blaster fire, and Kronock yells.

Jax stole a glance to his sides and the prisoners gathering. "There are more of us than there are of them. Are we together?"

The prisoners responded with yells of affirmation as they surged forward, clearly empowered by our numbers advantage and the possibility of escape.

Jax wrapped his free arm around me, holding me to his back. "Stay behind me, Samaira."

Hearing him use my name sent a strange thrill through me. I couldn't give up on Jax. Not after everything we'd been through. I reached into my suit and grabbed the blaster from the back of my waistband. "And let you have all the fun? No way."

Pivoting around his arm, I stood shoulder to shoulder with him and started shooting. "You shoot up, and I'll shoot down."

He glanced at me, his expression telling me that he

wasn't happy I was exposing myself to danger, but he must have known better than to argue with me. With a resigned nod, he aimed up while I aimed down, and we moved toward the stairs. I took a second to locate Fillian, grabbing him by the collar and keeping him tucked between me and Jax.

Once the prisoners joined us, it was hard to shoot around them, especially since several of them were considerably bigger than me. Before I could tell a beefy alien with purple skin to duck, he rushed at a Kronock, snatching the guard's baton and turning it on him before giving the creature a hard shove down the stairs. The Kronock took out several more guards on his way down, and then a flood of alien prisoners trampled on the bodies as they stampeded up from below.

"Faster," I cried to Jax, realizing that the flow of prisoners eager to get to the surface could easily crush us if we didn't pick up the pace.

His eyes widened, but he moved faster, jogging up the stairs as he fired a spray of laser fire at the incoming Kronock. A brief glance told me Fillian was still by my side, his purple hair now a bright shade of pink.

"I can't believe you actually came," he said, grinning up at me.

My smile to him vanished as the Gatazoid tripped on the stairs, his skinny legs slipping through the wide metal steps as he went down. All I could see was flashes of Rayan as he'd dropped beside me. I tried to stop and lunge for the little alien, but his hands were just past my reach. I was too terrified to scream as I watched his slight body start to fall.

No, no, no, no. I couldn't lose someone else. Not again. Fillian might not be Rayan, but he'd trusted me. Then Jax's large hand thrust between the metal steps and caught

Fillian, snatching him up from the dark, yawning space below.

I choked back a sob as Jax plopped Fillian beside me. The Gatazoid was shaking and looked shellshocked, but he wasn't hurt.

"We're all getting out," Jax said.

I couldn't do much more than nod and swallow hard as he bustled us both up the remaining few flights. It had been longer than I could remember when I'd been able to count on someone like I could clearly count on Jax, and I had to admit that I liked the feeling. Not having to be alone and do everything on my own was actually nice. A warm glow filled my chest as I thought about how many times Jax had saved my ass and how I didn't mind. In fact, I liked it. Then a chill swept over me as I remembered that I'd ruined it.

Once we were on the top landing and no more Kronock were coming from above, Jax pulled me to one side.

"I'll stay back and make sure everyone gets out," Jax said, dragging in a breath. "I'll meet you on the surface."

I glanced at the seemingly endless flow of prisoners swarming up from below. "I'm not leaving you down here."

His gaze narrowed and a muscle twitched in his jaw. "Sam."

I matched his stance. "I'm not leaving you behind. You may not want to be with me anymore but that doesn't mean we aren't a team. At least for now."

His brow furrowed for a beat then he nodded, even though his jaw remained tense. "We go together?"

"That's what teams do, right?" The phrase should have felt wrong on my lips, but it didn't. I trusted Jax. He wouldn't let me down, and I owed him the same loyalty. After all, he was the mission, and I still hadn't gotten him from Kronock space. Not yet. But if I was being honest, he was more than the mission. Maybe more than I was willing to admit.

I took my place beside the Drexian as the prisoners fled the dark confines of the deep prison. When the flow of aliens slowed to a trickle, the last ones hobbling or limping as they pulled themselves up by the metal railings, he peered down. "I think that may be everyone. Time for us to get the *grek* out."

"Then let's ditch this bloody place," I said.

Jax took a step toward the stairs, holding out his hand for me to take. Before I could slip my hand in his, a thick arm snatched me back from behind, tightening around my neck.

"I don't think so," the Kronock voice said, hot and grating in my ear.

CHAPTER

THIRTY-ONE

Jaxon

Fear iced my skin as I whirled around. An injured Kronock guard—his helmet askew and blood trickling from a blaster wound in his side—held Sam dangling from the crook of his arm. A grin curled his thin scaly lips as he squeezed his grip, and Sam clawed at his arms, her mouth opening and closing in desperation.

I leveled my blaster at him. "Drop her."

The stairs creaked and rattled, and the metal door overhead groaned as it slammed, making the dirt ceiling rain a fine mist of dust over us.

He hoisted her up so that she covered more of his head. "I'll snap her neck before you can get off a shot."

I wasn't sure if that was true, but the way he gripped her neck worried me. It wouldn't take much more pressure to kill her, and the Kronock didn't seem to have a problem with taking her down with him.

Thoughts raced through my head. I could take the head shot and hope that I didn't miss, but that could be a death sentence for Sam. I could try to take out his arm and hope that he dropped her in reaction, but there was also a chance he could move slightly, and I'd end up shooting her. There was no scenario in which Sam's safety was guaranteed —except one.

"Take me," I said.

The Kronock angled his long jaw at me, while Sam tried to jerk her head from side to side, her eyes wild. "A trade?"

I nodded, the fear that had been gnawing at my throat evaporating. If I could be sure Sam was safe, I didn't care what happened to me. I'd been tortured by the Kronock before. I could survive it again. But I couldn't bear the thought of Sam suffering the same fate. Not when I could prevent it.

The realization that I truly cared for her slammed into me, almost stealing my breath. I didn't want to let her go— not at the end of the mission and not ever. Which made what I had to do to save her even worse.

"That's right." I waved a hand dismissively at Sam. "A Drexian is more valuable than a puny human like this."

The Kronock faltered, relaxing his grip slightly. "A Drexian prisoner is a prize."

Sam gasped as her airway was freed. "No way. I won't let you—"

Her words were cut off as the Kronock jerked his arm back around her windpipe. I flinched at this, but she was still moving, which meant he hadn't inadvertently snapped her neck. But I couldn't count on getting lucky again. The alien brute had no idea of his strength and the frailty of the human body.

Dirt sifted down from above us, a dark powder settling on Sam's hair and the Kronock's scaled head.

I lowered my blaster slightly. "Let her go, and I'll come with you willingly."

Sam struggled, even as her face took on a purplish hue.

The Kronock glanced down at her, his beady eyes darting back to me. "Why? Is this human valuable?"

"Valuable?" I tried to scoff but it came out a choked cough. "She's just a human like all the others. Their planet has billions of them. Human females are a dime a dozen."

He didn't make a move to release her. "Then why not let this one die?" His lip curled into a sneer. "Is she your mate?" He inhaled deeply. "I can smell you on her."

Watching him breathe in the scent of Samaira made me grit my teeth, despising what I had to say next. "I fucked her. Why not? A Drexian will always fuck a willing female, but she's not my mate. I have no desire to take a human mate. I never have."

Sam stilled, her gaze locking onto me and her eyes glittering with tears, but I couldn't back down. Not if I wanted him to be convinced I didn't care for her. "I'm not like the rest of my Drexian brothers who're ruled by these weak creatures. I prefer battle and bedding many females. This one will be cast away just like the rest."

Sam twitched at this, something flashing across her eyes, but the Kronock guard let out a gurgling laugh. "I prefer fucking and killing anything that puts up a fight." He sniffed her neck again. "What's the fun in them being willing?"

"Call it a fetish." My fingers twitched with the desire to snap his neck. "She means nothing to me, but it will be a mar on my record if she dies under my watch."

His black eyes hardened. "You care about your record enough to take her place?"

"Drexian honor is everything," I said, speaking the truth to the monster for the first time. "Even dying at your hands is better than failing to save someone under my charge."

He shook his head brusquely, uncoiling his thick arm enough for Sam to suck in a breath. "I do not understand Drexians, but I am more than willing to take your life instead of hers."

"Then we have a deal?" I locked my gaze on Sam's, sending her a silent warning not to protest.

I hoped that she could also read the regret in my eyes for all the horrible lies I'd just spewed to gain her freedom, but there was only so much a single look could convey. If the fury blazing from her gaze was any indication, she either didn't know that I'd said what I had to convince the Kronock to release her, or she was livid at me for making the trade. Or both.

"Samaira," I whispered, just loud enough for her to hear. She recoiled a bit, but blinked rapidly, finally lowering her gaze for a beat and granting me a single, small nod.

"Kick your blaster to me," the Kronock said, coughing as more dirt fell from above.

Noises rose from deep within the subterranean complex, but they weren't alien or Kronock voices. They were the groans of metal buckling and the roar of rock collapsing.

Panic clutched my chest like a vise. The entire underground prison was collapsing from within—and we were inside it and beneath tons of dirt and rock.

Sam's furious expression morphed to one of pure terror, and even the Kronock holding her loosened the arm fastened around her neck, peering up as clods of dirt thudded around him.

"Impossible," he said, staggering back when an unusually large clump of dirt struck his helmet.

I didn't wait for Sam to be completely free. There was no time to worry about the Kronock breaking her neck. I darted forward while he was distracted, grasped her hand, and fired straight into the guard's face.

He dropped like a stone, his body littering the ground along with a growing collection of rocks and splattered clumps of hard-packed dirt.

"Come on!" I jerked her forward with me as the ceiling caved in behind us, blanketing the dead Kronock.

We made it to the metal stairs, but they were swaying as the walls they were anchored to crumbled apart. I chanced a glance below and could see the cavernous open space caving in on itself, the steel web of stairs collapsing in a deafening scream of grinding metal and crashing rock.

My heart thundered almost as loud as the cave-in as I gripped the railing and pulled Sam with me. Our only chance was to make it up the last bit of remaining staircase before it all got sucked into the collapse below. It was almost impossible to keep my balance as the stairs came apart beneath me, and I was knocked to my knees, Sam's hand slipping from mine.

I pushed myself up and spun around to grab her, but the

stair she was on fell away at her feet and she started to plummet into the roiling sinkhole.

"No!" I dove for her, grasping her hand before she dropped and then catching a railing to keep me from going over the edge.

Her eyes were wide as she hung over the abyss. "We'll both be pulled in. Let me go."

I shook my head. "I thought we agreed. We go together."

A tear leaked from the corner of her eye, then she clenched her jaw and hoisted her other hand up to clasp my arm. "Drexians really are the most stubborn pains in the arse."

I smiled at this, glad to hear the snark return to her voice. Then I used my other arm to pull us both back onto the small landing. We were so close to the door leading out that I could see the flash of the metal panel from the green glow of the few ambient lights still working. "Almost there."

I shifted Sam so that she was in front of me, my arms encircling her. No way was I going to let her slip away again. I didn't look back, but I could hear more metal railing ripping from the stone walls as we both heaved ourselves upon the last few stairs that were nearly vertical.

The top stairs were bolted into the wide metal door leading into the decimated underground complex, and that was the only reason they hadn't fallen into the collapse. The door was so close I could almost touch it. Only a couple more steps, and I'd be able to push it open.

Sam stretched one arm out, her fingertips brushing the steel push bar that extended from one side to the other. "I've got it!"

Then the remaining stairs disappeared beneath our feet,

the last lights flickered out, and with a loud roar, we were plunged into blackness.

CHAPTER
THIRTY-TWO

Samaira

I opened my eyes, but there was nothing but darkness and silence. Was this the afterlife? It didn't look like what I'd always imagined of Akhirah, the afterlife I'd been taught to believe in by my devoutly Muslim father. Inhaling, I could detect the loamy scent of soil. Not what the afterlife was supposed to smell like, either.

Had I died? The last thing I remembered was grabbing the bar of the door over my head, and then the stairs beneath my feet crumbling away. Jax had been right at my back, his arms coiled around my waist and tightening as the stairs had dropped.

My heart lurched. Jax. Where was he? I cleared my throat, coughing out remnant of the all the dust I'd inhaled as we'd raced up the stairs trying to escape. "Jax?"

My voice echoed back to me, and I realized that I was no longer in a cavernous underground complex. That was gone, and wherever I was much smaller. Panic sunk sharp talons in me as I shifted, lifting my hands overhead and hitting cool metal. The door!

With a surge of excitement, I pushed up, bracing myself for the light that would spill inside. But the metal didn't budge. It felt like the door was jammed. My heart raced as another thought struck me. If the entire complex had caved in, the door that had led outside must have collapsed as well. I might very well be hundreds of feet underground with tons of rubble covering the door.

I steadied my breath even as I fought the urge to scream. I'd never minded enclosed spaces, and I'd spent enough time in vents that being enclosed didn't bother me. But I'd always had a way out. I'd never been trapped underground with limited oxygen.

Stay calm, Samaira. Panic will only make you breathe faster and burn through your oxygen.

I shifted again, stretching out my arms and legs to see just how much space—and oxygen—I was dealing with. I could sit up and stretch my arms overhead. That was good. And I was resting on a metal step—maybe the top one?—with enough space to extend my legs all the way in front of me.

I swept one leg out, bumping something firm but not metallic. My pulse quickened, and I crawled over to the body crumpled at my feet. "Jax?"

My heart pounded as I moved my hands across his body in the dark until I found his face, kneeling until I felt the faint puff of warm breath on my cheek. He was breathing. I shook him gently, happiness surging through me that he'd survived and that he was with me.

"Sam?" he said groggily after a few seconds.

"I'm here." My voice cracked as I helped him sit up, propping him against me. "We survived."

"Did we?" He sounded skeptical.

I didn't blame him. We were in the dark, clearly buried under some amount of rubble. "Are you okay?"

He grunted. "My head hurts."

I moved my fingers across his face until I reached a sticky patch on the side of his head. Blood. I felt gingerly for a gash, but nothing was gaping or pulsing blood—both good signs. "I think you banged your head in the fall, but it's nothing serious."

"Easy for you to say," he grumbled.

I was so grateful for his complaints and the sound of his voice that I almost laughed. "I guess so."

"What happened? We'd reached the hatch to the outside, hadn't we?"

"We did, but then the stairs collapsed under our feet."

He groaned, sitting up. "How are we alive?"

I shifted as he moved his weight off me. "We're right under the hatch. That must have kept the rest of the dirt and rocks from caving in around us. But the hatch is covered by something. I already tried to push it open. No luck."

"They'll know we're under here," Jax said, his voice steely. "Fillian will know we were right behind him. The Drexians will find us."

I imagined Fillian on the surface as the underground

prison had collapsed with us inside it. Would he even entertain the possibility that we'd be alive? What was happening with all the alien prisoners, now that they were free on the surface of the black moon? They outnumbered any Kronock guards that had managed to escape, but would the Kronock know their prison had collapsed? Would they send reinforcements? Or had the Drexians detected my beacon ring and arrived with a fleet to rescue us? What I wanted to know most of all was how Jax maintained total confidence that we'd be saved.

"Do Drexians ever doubt?" I asked him.

There was a long stretch of silence between us. "Not in each other. I've never been betrayed by one of my brothers."

What was unspoken was that he had been let down before—and by me.

"I never meant to betray you, Jax. To me, none of it was fake."

His hand found my face in the dark. "I know. I shouldn't have said those things. I was angry and scared of losing you."

My heart stuttered in my chest. "I thought you didn't have any interest in humans." I recalled his words to the Kronock guard. "I thought we were a dime a dozen. I thought you preferred bedding lots of different alien females?"

He stilled, his hand twitching as he held my face. "Those were lies meant to save you. Nothing more."

"But you've told me before you never wanted a human mate. How do I know what to believe?"

He slid an arm around me, pulling me so I was body-to-body with him. "What do you feel, Samaira? What do I make you feel?"

I couldn't tell him that he made me feel things no one ever had or that when I was with him, I didn't feel so alone anymore. I couldn't admit that I'd been wrong to put walls around my heart or that his refusal to leave me and his offer to sacrifice his life for mine had battered those walls until they were as much useless rubble as what surrounded us. Or could I?

The chances of us getting out alive were slim. We were trapped in a small space and buried who knew how deep? Even if the Drexians did fly in with an entire fleet and beat back the Kronock, would they be able to dig us out before the dirt caved in around us, or our air ran out?

"You make me want to give it all up," I said, the words bubbling from me.

"Give what up?"

"The fear, the distrust, everything that's been holding me together and keeping me alone for so many years. Being with you makes me want to toss it all away."

"Then do." He dragged the rough pad of his thumb across my jawline. "Toss it all away, and I'll throw out my fear of being with one woman and risking getting my heart broken again."

I hitched in a breath. "But you were so mad at me."

"I was scared and hurt and stupid. When you left, all I could think about was the tribute who'd left me."

Of course. Why hadn't that occurred to me? I'd been so focused on dealing with my own demons and saving Fillian that I hadn't thought how it would feel to Jax. "I'm so sorry. I never meant—"

He rested his forehead against mine. "I know you didn't, and I know you're nothing like her. Although I'd like you to be like her in one way." He drew in a shaky breath. "Be my mate, Samaira."

My breaths were shallow as I processed his words. Tears stung the backs of my eyelids, and my throat squeezed. "Really? You're not just taking the piss?"

I should be panicking that Jax was moving so fast after only knowing each other a few days. It was crazy and impetuous—and it felt more right than anything. I'd never even imagined myself getting married, much less to a Drexian warrior. But I also couldn't imagine spending a minute of the rest of my life without the infuriating guy, even if the rest of my life was only going to be measured in minutes.

"I don't know what that means, but I'm serious, Samaira. I never want to lose you again."

"This might be the shortest engagement in history," I said, inhaling dust and coughing.

"Is that a yes?"

I laughed, even as my chest constricted from the thin air. "That's a yes. I shouldn't love you because you're a cocky Drexian who tries to boss me around."

He sucked in a short breath. "But you do, don't you?"

I rolled my eyes even though he couldn't see me doing it. "I do, but I'm sure you already assumed that didn't you?"

"I am cocky." He brushed his lips across mine. "And I also love you, even though you're stubborn and insist on doing everything yourself."

The oxygen was so low that my chest burned as I tried to snatch in breaths. Even though I was lightheaded, and my eyelids were drooping, a strange sense of contentment washed over me. I'd had to cross a galaxy, crash onto a black moon, get buried under tons of rubble, but I'd finally found what I'd been searching for my entire life. Even if I'd only fully embraced love for a matter of hours, I'd finally opened myself to it. I'd finally found *him*.

I let my eyes flutter shut, hearing him whisper my name as I sank into oblivion.

CHAPTER
THIRTY-THREE

Jaxon

The light wasn't bright, but it glowed through my eyelids, making me drape an arm over my face to block it.

"There they are!" The voice shrieking in the distance was vaguely familiar, but I shook it off. I'd been having such a nice dream about Sam.

She'd been with me in one of the fantasy suites on the Island. I'd never been inside one, but I'd heard plenty about the holographic wonderlands from my fellow Drexians. Even though I'd been determined never to set foot in one after I'd been rejected by my match, I'd been in one with Sam. We'd both been lounging in a pool of sorts, the crystal-blue water lapping against my back as I held Sam in my arms.

Sam!

I jerked back to reality at the thought of her, flinging my

arm off my face and blinking up into the light. Where was she?

"Samaira?" My voice came out as a wisp of a croak, my throat raw from breathing in dust and gasping for final breaths.

I put a hand to my temple, my head throbbing. We'd had no air. We'd both been stealing shallow, desperate breaths before I'd passed out. I forced myself to shift my head to the side. I'd been holding her, but now she was gone. She was no longer by my side.

Darkness threatened to engulf me again, but a strong hand clasped my own and pulled me up. I focused on the Drexian slipping an arm around my back to keep me upright, my eyes locking on the Inferno Force insignia on his uniform before I found his face—a familiar face. "Dryx?"

"Good to see you, Jax." He walked me over to the edge of the hole I stood in, grabbing a ring tied to a rope and slipping it over my head until it settled around my waist. "We thought we lost you."

Tipping my head back, I spotted a group of Drexians and aliens standing several meters above me. The Drexians held the other end of the rope holding me. I scanned the group but didn't see Sam. "What about Sam...the human female I was with?"

Dryx thumped me on the back. "We already pulled her out. You don't think we'd leave a pretty female behind, do you?"

Relief flooded me as I was hoisted from the rubble. Even though I couldn't see Sam, she was safe. That was what mattered.

I righted myself once I was on solid ground, holding out

my arms for balance. Glancing back, my stomach roiled. The earth that had once housed hundreds of prisoners was now a sunken pit with shards of metal jutting from the surface. It was a miracle Sam and I hadn't been sucked down into the depths of the rubble, the heavy hatch somehow protecting us and creating a pocket of air.

Overhead a blast of laser fire erupted, making me jump. A Kronock fighter swooped through the air but was blasted from the sky by an invisible shooter—a Drexian ship with stealth shielding. I felt like cheering.

"How—?"

Before I could ask what was going on, Vekron appeared at my side, his gaze scouring me. "You don't look great, but you're alive."

"Thanks. How did you...?"

He gave me a crooked smile as he ran his hand through his loose, dark hair. "How do you think? I'm assuming you and Sam activated the beacon ring on purpose."

I nodded, not wanting to admit that I'd had my doubts about the gadget. "You picked up the signal?"

"As soon as you sent it. It took us a few jumps to get to you, but once we pinpointed the moon, it didn't take long to find the action." His expression darkened. "I had no idea the Kronock had black moons—or prisons on them."

"When we crashed, we had no idea about the prison. The Kronock kept it well hidden."

Vekron's gaze dropped. "We found the ship and the bodies of the rest of the crew."

"They died heroes' deaths in battle."

"They've already been transferred to the Inferno Force battleship. They'll get warriors burials."

I flicked my gaze to the sky. "There's an Inferno Force battleship here?"

"More than one." Vekron also looked up. "Once we had the beacon, we could lock onto the coordinates and jump the fleet in. It didn't take long to take out the Kronock battleship. We're just finishing up with the remaining enemy fighters."

"They didn't send reinforcements?"

"We struck hard and fast." Vekron's voice swelled with pride. "Either the Kronock couldn't send out a distress call, or their forces decided not to risk any more ships against us."

That sounded like the Kronock. They would easily sacrifice a battleship and countless soldiers if it meant they wouldn't suffer further losses. And in their weakened state, I suspected they couldn't afford to lose any more ships or soldiers.

"I'm glad you took out the enemy quickly. We wouldn't have lasted much longer underground." I suppressed a shudder at the memory of being trapped in the dark. "How did you know where to find us? We left the beacon in the middle of the jungle to draw the enemy away from the prison."

"The collapse of the underground complex set off quakes all over the moon. We knew something was going on. We just didn't know exactly what until we saw all the aliens rushing up from the ground like Crillian fire ants emerging from a hill. Dryx took the first fighter down to the surface and your friend told him what had happened and insisted he start digging."

"My friend?"

"The Gatazoid." Vekron's mouth twitched. "He's pretty

forceful for a little guy. I'm starting to think it isn't just a Serge thing. It's a species thing."

It was hard to imagine Fillian being forceful, but I was glad he had been. I rested a hand on Vekron's shoulder. "Thank you for coming."

He scoffed at this but smiled. "We're Inferno Force. When do we ever leave a Drexian behind?" He paused and gave me a pointed look. "Or a human?"

My face warmed at his knowing gaze. "Where is she?"

He stepped back, waving an arm in the direction of a Drexian medical officer who stood beside Sam, waving a scanning device over her. Fillian stood on the other side of Sam, eyeing the scanner and the Drexian with suspicion.

The moment I saw Sam, my heart squeezed. If my head wasn't swimming and my body aching, I would have run to her. But then I hesitated. We'd said a lot of things to each other, but we'd also thought we were dying. I'd meant every word of what I'd said, including asking her to be my mate. But had she meant what she'd said?

I hated that doubt was creeping into my mind, but it was one thing to profess love and agree to be someone's mate after careful consideration and deliberation, and it was another to do it when you didn't think you'd live long enough to see through any of those promises.

I was bracing myself for the inevitable cool and awkward reception from Sam when she looked up and spotted me. Her face lit up, and she rushed toward me, throwing her arms around me so hard I staggered back and almost fell.

"You're okay," she said, her voice choked with emotion. "I thought we were both done for."

"I'm okay." I wrapped my arms around her, the feel of her body against mine sending pulses of heat through me. "You did it, Sam. You completed your mission."

She pulled back from me, studying my face for a second. "You're way more than my mission by now." She cocked one eyebrow. "Unless I imagined it, you're my fiancé."

A thrill went through me so hard I jerked. Then I tightened my grip on her. "If you'll still have me."

She cut her eyes to the Drexians around us, giving me a mischievous grin. "Oh, I plan to have you, Jax. As many ways and as much as possible."

This sent a rumble of laughter through me. "And I thought males were the ones who had one thing on their mind?"

She stroked one hand down the side of my face. "I have lots of things on my mind, but almost all of them involve you and me together—with very little clothing."

"What about going back to Earth?" I asked, hating that the question still lingered in the back of my brain.

"You mean the place where I'm considered a criminal?" She frowned. "I'd rather take my chances out here in space. Besides, it seems like the Drexians can use someone with my skill set."

"If you think I'm going to let you go off on any more dangerous missions—"

"Relax, tough guy. I meant that they could use me to teach your warriors." She tilted her head at me. "And what about you returning to Inferno Force?"

"Who says Inferno Force doesn't need someone to teach them skills like yours?"

Sam kissed me hard. "Now that's a plan I can get behind, and you know I love a good plan."

"I know." I kissed her back, but deeply, letting my lips claim hers as she moaned into me.

CHAPTER

THIRTY-FOUR

Samaira

I rolled over, opening my eyes and taking in the glowing streaks of blue, purple, and pink light that illuminated the glass dome overhead. The colors undulated across the dark sky, as if they were being continuously painted by a celestial brush. I draped my arm across Jax's bare chest as he heaved in lungfuls of air, my hand slipping on the damp skin.

"I never imagined that we would be here," he said, curling the arm that was under me, and tugging me so that I was pulled on top of him.

My heart beat like a tripwire as I tried to catch my breath. "I never thought I'd make love under the northern lights, either. It's incredible."

He let out a small chuckle. "That is not what I meant, but these northern lights from Earth are mesmerizing. I never imagined I'd be staying in one of the fantasy suites on the Island."

I cast my gaze around the low bed covered in fluffy, white, faux-fur blankets, and the fireplace crackling at the far end of the suite. Designed to replicate the clear-domed, glass igloos in Scandinavia that gave picture perfect views of the aurora borealis, our holographic fantasy suite had the advantage of not being frigid or in the middle of nowhere.

Remnants of our dinner from the night before remained on a low table in front of the hearth, along with an empty bottle of Palaxian wine. The fake bearskin rug stretched across the glossy wooden floor and the sunken hot tub bubbled away in the corner of the room next to the door to the cedar plank sauna, the scent of eucalyptus managing to fill the air.

"It's only temporary," I reminded him. "We can't stay here forever."

He tugged the edge of one of the furs over my bare ass. "Too bad. I could get used to living like the tribute brides do."

I instinctively wrinkled my nose. "I might have agreed to be the mate of a Drexian warrior, but that doesn't make me a tribute bride."

A rumbly laugh made his body shake. "No, it doesn't, and I pity the Drexian who dares call you one."

"No offense to the actual tribute brides," I added, trying to be less judgmental. After all, I *had* fallen for a Drexian despite my best efforts not to, so I didn't have much room to talk.

"Of course not."

I heard the mocking tone in Jax's voice and slapped his

chest. "Hey, I'm trying."

He slipped one hand under the fur and squeezed my ass. "Your enthusiastic efforts are appreciated."

"Cocky git," I muttered, fighting to keep from smiling.

"What was that?" Jax rolled over, flipping me onto my back. He pinned my hands over my head while holding himself between my legs.

I gave him a look of challenge, raising one eyebrow. "You heard me, mate."

His lips quirked as he shifted so that his still-hard cock was notched at my opening. "These words you keep using aren't like the Earth words I'm used to."

"That's because you've been around too many Americans."

He tilted his head. "I know there are different languages on Earth, but I thought you spoke the same language as the Americans."

I bobbled my head. "Kind of."

He narrowed his eyes, but his grin didn't falter. "You are still maddening, Samaira."

My heart did a somersault at the sound of my name on his lips. "You're the only one who can call me that, you know."

He shifted his weight, pressing his thick crown inside me. "Good. And I'm the only one who can do this to you."

"Mmhmmm," I hummed, my eyelids fluttering as his rigid length slowly filled me. Since Drexians didn't go soft after coming or need time to recuperate, Jax could go all night—a fact I'd personally tested on the bearskin rug.

I wrapped my legs around his waist as he started moving inside me. I was already slick from his seed, and the thought sent a strange thrill through me. When he loosened his grip on my hands and bent over me, I rocked my body hard to one side, pushing him onto his back and straddling him.

His eyes were wide, as he grasped my hips and peered up at me. "You wish to ride me?"

My only answer was a sly grin as I braced my feet next to his hips and started to move up and down the length of his cock. Jax arched his back and tipped his head back, groaning as I bounced up and down.

When he looked back at me, his gaze was hot, and it traveled down my body until he was watching where our bodies joined. "You take me so well."

"We fit," I said with a slow smile.

Sliding one hand around from my hip, he found my clit and circled it as I continued to ride him. "We do, indeed. I want to watch you come on my cock, Samaira."

Tremors of pleasure vibrated through my body. I wanted him to watch me, his gaze on me ratcheting up my arousal. As my breathing became ragged, I took my breasts in my own hands, rolling my nipples between my fingers.

Jax emitted a throaty growl, his gaze molten as he watched me.

"You like to watch me touch myself?" I asked, my voice breathy.

He clenched his jaw, working his finger faster over my clit as he met each of my thrusts onto his cock with one of his own. Then he reached up and took one of my hands, dragging it down and placing it on my clit. He used my own fingers underneath his to work my swollen nub. "I like feeling you touch yourself."

With a desperate gasp, I threw my head back, sensations

storming through me like a torrent bursting through the floodgates. My body spasmed as I clenched around his cock, screaming and rocking until I fell forward, catching myself before I flopped onto his chest.

Jax didn't miss a beat, flipping me over onto my hands and knees, jerking my ass high into the air and spreading my legs before thrusting hard and deep. I was still shuddering from my orgasm, and my body clamped around him as he pistoned fast into me. Within seconds, he was arching back and roaring as he exploded inside me, his fingers biting into my flesh as he held onto me. Then he slumped over me, resting his cheek on my back while we both sucked in air.

After a few minutes of our suite being filled with the sounds of heavy breathing, Jax collapsed on the bed next to me, and I sank down onto my belly, my legs quivering.

"How long do we get to stay here again?" I asked once I could speak. "Because I'm not sure when I'll be able to walk again."

Jax rolled his head over to look at me, his smile wide. "Maybe if I keep fucking you like that, they'll let us stay once the tribute brides arrive."

"Are you going to explain that I can't walk because you've fucked me so hard?"

"That's exactly what I'll say."

I rolled my eyes. "Cocky prat."

Jax rolled over so that he was facing me. "You love me for being such a cocky..."

"Prat," I finished for him. "And I love you *in spite* of that."

He pulled my face to his and kissed me. "As long as you love me."

As bizarre as it was that I'd fallen so hard and so fast for the last guy I ever could have imagined, I did love Jax. Despite me calling him cocky—and meaning it most of the time—he was also loyal and devoted and honorable. Not to mention sexy as hell with a body that still made my mouth go dry. He'd earned my trust and devotion on the black moon, risking his life for me and all the prisoners.

As we lay side by side soaking in the stunning views overhead, a beep pulled me from my daze.

"Who could be at our door?" Jax asked, pushing himself up onto his elbows.

"Maybe it's breakfast." I didn't have much of a sense of time, and because our suite was holographic and it was always night with the northern lights shimmering, it could be the middle of the station's ship cycle for all I knew.

"We do need to replenish." Jax eyed the decimated dinner on the table before bellowing, "Come in!"

But it wasn't breakfast being delivered—or lunch.

"Still in bed?" Serge asked, bustling into the room in a peacock-blue suit with bright-green shoes that rapped a staccato beat on the floor. Behind him was Fillian, dressed more modestly in a dark-blue outfit without flared lapels.

"Fillian?" Jax rubbed his eyes, as if he wasn't sure he was seeing correctly.

"Apologies for the intrusion," Fillian said, his hair beginning to flush pink at the roots.

"Intrusion?" Serge cut his eyes to his fellow Gatazoid and then back to us. "We aren't intruding. We're here to get vital information."

"What's going on?" Jax's voice sharpened. "Is it the Kronock? Is it the station?"

Serge flapped a hand at him. "No, everything's fine with

the station, and we haven't heard a blip from those awful Kronock since you all returned and closed the energy rift. We're here about the cake."

Now I rubbed my head. "The cake?"

Serge huffed out a long breath, while Fillian shifted from foot to foot. "The wedding cake. Your wedding cake. Since Fillian here has agreed to become the Island's exclusive wedding cake baker, we need to get working on the design of your cake."

"Our wedding cake?" Jax asked.

Serge shook his head, his expression conveying his overall impatience. "You are getting married, aren't you? I do have a wedding to plan, don't I?"

"Well, yes," I said.

"Then we need a cake." Serge gave a definitive nod of his head. "I watched your Earth documentary, *Father of the Bride*. For one, it made me glad I don't deal with parents of tribute brides, but more importantly, I learned that the design of the entire event hinges around the cake."

"The cake?" Jax repeated.

Serge gave me a pointed look. "Is he having some sort of delayed response from being deprived of oxygen in that prison collapse?"

"We can always discuss this later," Fillian said, giving me a tentative smile. "I'm glad to see you're both okay."

I smiled back at the Gatazoid. I'd heard he'd been welcomed onto the station with open arms by Serge, who was thrilled to have another member of his species on board. Fillian had already gained weight in the few days we'd been back, and his cheeks were no longer sunken, nor was his skin so pale. "I'm glad to see you've found a place here."

The prisoners from the Kronock prison moon had all been transported to the Island and were being given jobs or returned to their home worlds. I was chuffed that I'd played a part in saving them, but I was happiest about Fillian's new home.

"Fillian is a find," Serge said in a hushed voice, as if the cake baker might be poached away at any moment. "Frankly, even the Boat will have a hard time competing with his talent. Especially if Sid keeps insisting on cauliflower icing."

I grimaced. "I can say for sure that I don't want cauliflower icing."

"That's a start, I suppose," Serge said.

"And that's where it will have to end for now," Jax said, standing and letting the furs fall off him.

Serge's round eyes nearly popped from his head, and he yelped as he attempted to avert his eyes from the long cock hanging between Jax's legs. "Perhaps we should come back later." He stumbled back with one hand shielding his eyes, walking in a circuitous path toward the door. "Let's go, Fillian. We'll try later."

"Maybe next week," Jax said, watching them trip over each other trying to leave the room and pressing the side panel to close the door.

"Next week?" I teased, as Jax strode back to the bed. It was all I could do not to gape at his hardening cock.

He gave me a wicked grin, lowering himself onto the bed and crawling up. "It will take at least that long to do all the things I have planned for you. And maybe another week for you to recover."

I wrapped my hands around his neck as my pulse fluttered. "So cocky."

EPILOGUE

Nina

"I've never been on an Inferno Force battleship before." I shifted my crossbody bag on my shoulder as I followed Vekron through the dimly lit corridor of the vessel.

Unlike the space station, the Inferno Force ship was not pulsing pink light and sleek, white surfaces. It was gritty and utilitarian—all dark iron and black walls with exposed piping. The ship rattled and clanged as warriors moved throughout it, heavy boots pounding on the steel floors.

Vekron glanced back over his shoulder at me. The brown hair he often wore in a man bun was loose around his shoulders. "There isn't much need for them to visit holographic space stations. But since the fleet was called in to aid with the Kronock attack, this is the perfect time to add some holographic components to the battleship."

I eyed a pair of intense warriors passing, their dark hair shaggy and tattoos emblazoned down their arms. Leather straps crossed their bare chests, which glistened with sweat. They thumped their fists to their chests as they passed Vekron and nodded to me, their gazes moving quickly down my body.

My cheeks warmed at the less-than-subtle attention. It wasn't something I'd ever get used to, but Drexians were far less concerned about masking their arousal than humans were, and for some reason their gaze never felt creepy. Probably because they were so damn honorable. Drexian males would never dream of touching a female who was uninterested in them. Not without suffering serious consequences.

The Drexian warriors on the Island were used to seeing me and the other human women working on the station, so they no longer looked at us with such open curiosity. But these Inferno Force warriors weren't accustomed to females on their ship, and from what Vekron had told me, they'd been in deep space for a while.

"Have the Inferno Force warriors not gotten to change after the battle?" I asked, after another sweaty warrior walked by, this one with a red welt across his chest.

Vekron swiveled his head to me again, his lips twitching. "Since the ship isn't on a mission anymore, the warriors are enjoying some recreation."

"What kind of recreation leaves you so scarred?"

"Either Captain Brok has been challenging warriors on the *Kranji* mat, or they're engaged in traditional Drexian sparring."

"*Kranji*?"

"An alien martial art." Vekron paused at a doorway. "Very challenging."

"More challenging than the Drexian sparring I've seen that uses those sharp curved blades?"

"If Captain Brok is your opponent, yes." Vekron pressed his hand to a side panel and the door swished open. "That's what we're going to be working on. If we can install some basic holographic sensors, we can turn one of the sparring rings into a holodeck. Then the warriors can practice battling different opponents."

"Yippee," I deadpanned.

Vekron laughed as we entered the sparring ring, the scent of sweat so pungent I could almost taste it. "Inferno Force warriors enjoy battle. It's why we joined the elite unit."

I knew Vekron was part of Inferno Force, and that he was a tough fighter, but since I'd been working with him on the Island, I'd mostly seen his brilliant, tech-savvy side. He was the one who was a genius with devices and a master at simplifying holographic code. It was hard to picture him like the sweaty, hulking warriors stalking around the ship.

The moment the thought of Vekron sweaty and shirtless entered my mind, my pulse fluttered.

Come on, Nina. I almost sighed out loud. *He doesn't think of you like that. Vekron is your friend. Nothing more.*

Okay, at most he was my work husband, since we'd spent so much time together during the construction of the space station, but that still didn't mean he thought of me as anything more than that. Even if I'd spent way too much time thinking about him *without* his dark, Drexian uniform.

"Focus, Nina," I whispered to myself as I trailed behind Vekron into the empty battle ring. *You're here to help Vekron*

*add the holographic sensors to the Inferno Force ship and then
head back to the station. Nothing else.*

Vekron craned his neck around as he led me past the
enclosed battle cage encased in heavy iron chain link.
"What?"

"Nothing." I inclined my head at the cage. "Just
wondering if that's blood staining the mat."

Vekron gave me a wolfish grin, his pupils flaring, and for
the first time I saw a glimpse of the deadly warrior I knew he
must be to have made it into Inferno Force. My heart raced,
and I averted my gaze back to the sparring enclosure.

I tried not to think about the fact that he'd soon be
leaving the Island. The construction was almost complete,
and the tribute brides from Earth would be arriving, which
meant the permanent Drexian crew would also be arriving
and taking over. The Inferno Force warriors were only ever
meant to be temporary, although it was hard to think of the
space station I knew without them.

I hadn't decided if I would stay or not. My original
contract was for the construction, but they did need holographic designers to remain on the Island. Zoey, my best
friend on the station, had never planned to stay past the
christening, but now that she'd fallen head over heels for
the acting captain, Kalex, they were both considering
staying.

"So, what do you think, Nina?"

I jerked my head to Vekron, realizing we were standing in
front of an open panel, and he'd clearly been asking me a
question. "I think...definitely."

He cocked his head. "Definitely?"

Before I could let loose a string of Spanish curses in my

head, a siren sounded overhead and made me jump. "What's going on?"

Vekron glanced at the red flashing lights bouncing off the gray metal of the room, putting his palm to the wall. "I'm not sure, but the engines are powering up."

"As in to fly away?" I shook my head. "The ship can't leave. The captain knows we're on board, right?"

Vekron started jogging toward the door. "He knows."

I followed closely at my friend's heels, although I hated jogging, especially through a battleship as warriors rushed by us, tugging on uniform jackets. It didn't take us long to run up a few flights of stairs and a couple of ramps to reach the bridge, but if I'd thought the corridors were bustling with activity, the command deck was in chaos.

An imposing Drexian with short hair and a scar down one cheek stood with his legs braced wide as he looked out over the warriors standing at black consoles. Static and beeps punctuated the air as Drexians called out readings and incoming transmissions.

"Stay here," Vekron said, holding his arm in front of me and then striding forward to join the captain.

The Drexian, who was clearly in charge, turned to him, his expression registering surprise as Vekron thumped a fist over his heart. "Vekron?"

"Captain Brok, what's going on, sir?"

"There's been an attack on the Gerron colony. They've sent a call for help."

Vekron's jaw tensed. "The Kronock?"

"We don't know, but what we do know is that after the distress call, we lost all communication with them. We're preparing to jump in."

Vekron cut his eyes to me. "The human female and I were supposed to return to the Island before your departure."

"There's no time to get you on a transport ship now. Not if we want to save the colony." The captain pivoted on his heel, taking in the sight of me standing at the back of the bridge. "Sorry for the change in plans. Welcome to Inferno Force."

Then he turned back around and gave the orders to jump.

THANK YOU FOR READING **SCORCH!** Want to know what happens to Nina after she's trapped on the Inferno Force ship? Don't miss BURN, the third book in the Inferno Force series, featuring Vekron and Nina.

I was never supposed to be in the middle of an Inferno Force rescue mission. Or fall for the one Drexian warrior who's off-limits.

Life among the gorgeous warriors is anything but simple, and my feelings for my friend Vekron make it torturous. Even though we're forced together on the crowded spaceship, I can't let myself give in to my desires. Or can I?

One-click BURN

This book has been edited and proofed, but typos are like little gremlins that like to sneak in when we're not looking. If you spot a typo, please report it to: tana@tanastone.com
Thank you!!

PREVIEW OF BURN: INFERNO FORCE OF THE DREXIAN WARRIORS #3

Vekron

I glanced back as I led Nina through the dimly lit corridor of the gritty battleship.

"I've never been on an Inferno Force battleship before." She shifted the leather crossbody bag that crossed her chest and bisected her brightly colored, floral top, giving me a tentative smile.

I smiled back, taking in the mane of untamed curls spilling over her shoulders, and the glasses she pushed up her nose when she was nervous, like she was doing now. I didn't blame her for being a bit uneasy. This ship was a far cry from the station from which we'd just taken a transport.

Unlike the space station we'd flown over from, the Inferno Force ship wasn't all soft light and gleaming, white surfaces. It was functional and battle-scarred, with dark iron and exposed piping. It rattled and clanged as warriors moved throughout it, the clatter of heavy boots pounding on the steel floors comforting to me after so long spent aboard the sleek space station.

It wasn't that I'd missed the smell of sweat and engine fuel, but the sounds and smells of the battleship had defined a big part of my life. Breathing in the slightly humid air reminded me that I'd only been on loan to the Island. My real place was with Inferno Force, like my father and brother before me.

"There isn't much need for them to visit holographic space stations," I told Nina, forcing unwanted thoughts of my family from my head. "But since the fleet was called in to aid with the Kronock attack, this is the perfect time to add some holographic components to the battleship."

I eyed a pair of warriors passing, leather straps crossed their bare chests, which glistened with sweat. They thumped their fists to their chests as they passed me, and I returned their salute. Then I followed their gazes that lingered on the human female behind me. On the Drexian space station, Nina was notable for her bold style. Here, her loudly patterned clothing and wild hair drew stares. I felt an uneasy pang as I realized it was probably more than her clothes they were noticing.

Since we worked side by side, I'd conditioned myself not to think about Nina's soft curves or the way her hips swished when she walked. I'd all but steeled myself to the sweet scent of her hair and the flutter of her dark eyelashes. But these Inferno Force warriors had no such defenses, and they hadn't seen females in long enough that they looked at her like hungry predators. I squared my shoulders, giving the passing warriors severe looks as I pivoted in an attempt to block their view of Nina with my body.

I was being protective of her like a thoughtful colleague should be, I told myself. Then dirty images flashed into my brain of Nina splayed out beneath me wearing nothing but her shy smile. Okay, maybe it was more than that. I scowled at my weakness, reminding myself that Nina and I worked together, and I didn't want to mess up my work life because I couldn't stop thinking about her in a way I definitely shouldn't be.

Friends. Only friends.

"Have the Inferno Force warriors not gotten to change after the battle?" she asked after another sweaty warrior walked by, this one with a red welt across his chest.

I pulled my attention back to reality and fought back a grin at her obvious surprise at the Inferno Force warriors' lack of clothing and my satisfaction that her reaction to them hadn't been more carnal. "Since the ship isn't on a mission anymore, the warriors are enjoying some recreation."

"What kind of recreation leaves you so scarred?"

"Either Captain Brok has been challenging warriors on the *Kranji* mat, or they're engaged in traditional Drexian sparring."

"*Kranji?*"

"An alien martial art." I paused at a doorway. "Very challenging."

"More challenging than the Drexian sparring I've seen that uses those sharp, curved blades?"

"If Captain Brok is your opponent, yes." I thought about the times I'd gone up against the captain and come out with welts of my own. I pressed my hand to a side panel and the door swished open. "That's what we're going to be working on. If we can install some basic holographic sensors, we can turn one of the sparring rings into a holo-deck. Then the warriors can practice battling different opponents."

"Yippee," Nina deadpanned.

I laughed as we entered the sparring ring, the scent of sweat so familiar it was almost comforting. "Inferno Force warriors enjoy battle. It's why we joined the elite unit."

Nina whispered something I couldn't make out as we walked past the enclosed battle cage encased in heavy, iron, chain link. "What?"

"Nothing." She tipped her head at the cage. "Just wondering if that's blood staining the mat."

I gave her another grin without answering directly, my mind recalling the matches I'd fought with my Inferno Force brothers and my pulse quickening. She darted her gaze away as faint pink splotches appeared on her cheeks.

Seeing her blush made me smile wider and my heart stutter in my chest. I'd miss Nina getting flustered almost as much as I'd miss her sharp wit. I'd never worked with a female before—and certainly not a human female—but I'd grown to appreciate her intelligence and creativity. We'd made a good team, and her easy banter had made the workdays fly by. Trying to resist getting aroused by her had not made them easy though.

I tried not to think about the fact that I'd soon be leaving the Island and returning to Inferno Force. The construction was almost complete, and the tribute brides from Earth would be arriving, which meant the permanent Drexian crew would also be arriving and taking over. The Inferno Force warriors were only ever meant to be temporary, although it was hard to think of leaving the space station I'd worked so hard to create.

Even Nina wasn't sure if she would stay on the space station. Her contract had been for the construction, but now that her closest female friend on the Island had fallen for the captain, maybe she'd stay, too. I put this thought out of my mind. If Nina stayed, I'd be tempted to extend my contract as well. There were always more things to fix on a new station, and I hated the thought of leaving all that work to my friend. A friend who made my heart hammer, a small voice said in the back of my head.

I gave my head a brusque shake. Staying on the Island wasn't my destiny, no matter how much I enjoyed the challenge of the work. I was an Inferno Force warrior, which meant I served on battleships and fought off the Kronock. Making a name for myself and carrying on my family's legacy was more important than my personal desires. It always had been.

I paused in front of the panel that held all the wiring for the room, flipping it open and appraising the mess of wires. "I think we can use some of the existing wiring to piggyback the holographic system onto."

I glanced back when Nina didn't answer, noting that she had a far-away look in her eyes. "So, what do you think, Nina?"

She jerked her head up, blinking rapidly. "I think...definitely."

I cocked my head, almost certain she'd had no clue what I'd asked her. "Definitely?"

Before she could answer, a siren sounded overhead.

She jumped, pressing a hand to her heart. "What's going on?"

I cut my eyes to the red, flashing lights bouncing off the

metal walls, slapping a palm to the wall. "I'm not sure, but the engines are powering up."

"As in to fly away?" Nina shook her head. "The ship can't leave. The captain knows we're on board, right?"

I hurried toward the door. "He knows."

Nina managed to keep up as I nearly ran through the battleship, as warriors rushed by us tugging on uniform jackets. It didn't take us long to run up a few flights of stairs and a couple of ramps to reach the bridge, but if I'd thought the corridors were bustling with activity, the command deck was in chaos. Static and beeps punctuated the air as Drexians called out readings and incoming transmissions.

I spotted Captain Brok with his legs braced wide and his hands clasped behind his back.

"Stay here," I told Nina, holding one arm out in front of her and then striding forward to join the captain.

Captain Brok registered surprise when he saw me. "Vekron?"

"Captain Brok, what's going on, sir?"

"There's been an attack on the Gerron colony. They've sent a call for help."

I clenched my jaw as my body tingled with the anticipation of battle. "The Kronock?"

"We don't know, but we know that after the distress call, we lost all communication with them. We're preparing to jump in."

I slid my gaze to Nina, who stood wide-eyed amid the frantic preparations for war. "The human female and I were supposed to return to the Island before your departure."

"There's no time to get you on a transport ship, now. Not if we want to save the colony." The captain pivoted on his heel, taking in the sight of Nina standing at the back of the bridge. "Sorry for the change in plans. Welcome to Inferno Force."

Then he turned back around and gave the orders to jump.

to keep reading> One-click

Also by Tana Stone

Warriors of the Drexian Academy:

LEGACY

LOYALTY

Inferno Force of the Drexian Warriors:

IGNITE (also available on AUDIO)

SCORCH (also available on AUDIO)

BURN (also available on AUDIO)

BLAZE (also available on AUDIO)

FLAME (also available on AUDIO)

COMBUST

The Tribute Brides of the Drexian Warriors Series:

TAMED (also available in AUDIO)

SEIZED (also available in AUDIO)

EXPOSED (also available in AUDIO)

RANSOMED (also available in AUDIO)

FORBIDDEN (also available in AUDIO)

BOUND (also available in AUDIO)

JINGLED (A Holiday Novella) (also in AUDIO)

CRAVED (also available in AUDIO)

STOLEN (also available in AUDIO)

SCARRED (also available in AUDIO)

ALIEN & MONSTER ONE-SHOTS:

ROGUE (also available in AUDIO)

VIXIN: STRANDED WITH AN ALIEN

SLIPPERY WHEN YETI

CHRISTMAS WITH AN ALIEN

YOOL

Raider Warlords of the Vandar Series:

POSSESSED (also available in AUDIO)

PLUNDERED (also available in AUDIO)

PILLAGED (also available in AUDIO)

PURSUED (also available in AUDIO)

PUNISHED (also available on AUDIO)

PROVOKED (also available in AUDIO)

PRODIGAL (also available in AUDIO)

PRISONER

PROTECTOR

PRINCE

The Barbarians of the Sand Planet Series:

BOUNTY (also available in AUDIO)

CAPTIVE (also available in AUDIO)

TORMENT (also available on AUDIO)

TRIBUTE (also available as AUDIO)

SAVAGE (also available in AUDIO)

CLAIM (also available on AUDIO)

CHERISH: A Holiday Baby Short (also available on AUDIO)

PRIZE (also available on AUDIO)

SECRET

RESCUE (appearing first in PETS IN SPACE #8)

THE SKY CLAN OF THE TAORI:

SUBMIT (also available in AUDIO)

STALK (also available on AUDIO)

SEDUCE (also available on AUDIO)

SUBDUE

STORM

All the TANA STONE books available as audiobooks!

INFERNO FORCE OF THE DREXIAN WARRIORS:

IGNITE on AUDIBLE

SCORCH on AUDIBLE

BURN on AUDIBLE

BLAZE on AUDIBLE

FLAME on AUDIBLE

RAIDER WARLORDS OF THE VANDAR:

POSSESSED on AUDIBLE

PLUNDERED on AUDIBLE

PILLAGED on AUDIBLE

PURSUED on AUDIBLE

PUNISHED on AUDIBLE

PROVOKED on AUDIBLE

BARBARIANS OF THE SAND PLANET

BOUNTY on AUDIBLE

CAPTIVE on AUDIBLE

TORMENT on AUDIBLE

TRIBUTE on AUDIBLE

SAVAGE on AUDIBLE

CLAIM on AUDIBLE

CHERISH on AUDIBLE

TRIBUTE BRIDES OF THE DREXIAN WARRIORS

TAMED on AUDIBLE

SEIZED on AUDIBLE

EXPOSED on AUDIBLE

RANSOMED on AUDIBLE

FORBIDDEN on AUDIBLE

BOUND on AUDIBLE

JINGLED on AUDIBLE

CRAVED on AUDIBLE

STOLEN on AUDIBLE

SCARRED on AUDIBLE

SKY CLAN OF THE TAORI

SUBMIT on AUDIBLE

STALK on AUDIBLE

SEDUCE on AUDIBLE

About the Author

Tana Stone is a bestselling sci-fi romance author who loves sexy aliens and independent heroines. Her favorite superhero is Thor (with Aquaman a close second because, well, Jason Momoa), her favorite dessert is key lime pie (okay, fine, *all* pie), and she loves Star Wars and Star Trek equally. She still laments the loss of *Firefly*.

She has one husband, two teenagers, and two neurotic cats. She sometimes wishes she could teleport to a holographic space station like the one in her tribute brides series (or maybe vacation at the oasis with the sand planet barbarians). :-)

She loves hearing from readers! Email her any questions or comments at tana@tanastone.com.

Want to hang out with Tana in her private Facebook group? Join on all the fun at: https://www.facebook.com/groups/tanastonestributes/

Copyright © 2021 by Broadmoor Books

Cover Design by Croco Designs

Editing by Tanya Saari

All rights reserved.

No part of this book may be reproduced in any form or by any electronic or mechanical means, including information storage and retrieval systems, without written permission from the author, except for the use of brief quotations in a book review.

This is a work of fiction. Names, characters, places, and incidents are the products of the author's imagination or are used fictitiously and are not to be construed as real. Any resemblance to actual events, locales, organizations, or persons, living or dead, is entirely coincidental.

Printed in Dunstable, United Kingdom

66032196R00143